"That's what I want from you always, Tara. Lots of fire and spirit. I'm never at my best around yes people."

"That's rubbish, Max, and you know it. You love yes people. I hear you on the phone all the time, giving orders and expecting to be instantly obeyed. You like being the boss, in the bedroom as well as everywhere else! You expect all your lackeys to do exactly what they're told, when they're told."

"Aah, yes, but you're not one of my lackeys."

"I'm not so sure," she snapped. "Isn't a mistress another form of lackey?"

"Mistress! Good Lord, what a delightfully old-fashioned word. But I like it. Mistress," he repeated thoughtfully. "Yes, you would make me a perfect mistress."

MISTRESS TO A MILLIONAIRE

*She's his in the bedroom,
but he can't buy her love.*

The ultimate fantasy becomes a reality.

Live the dream with more
MISTRESS TO A MILLIONAIRE titles
by some of your much loved
Harlequin Presents® authors.

Watch for the next title in December 2004.
#2438 *The Billionaire's Pregnant Mistress*
by Lucy Monroe

Miranda Lee

THE MAGNATE'S MISTRESS

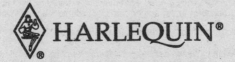

TORONTO • NEW YORK • LONDON
AMSTERDAM • PARIS • SYDNEY • HAMBURG
STOCKHOLM • ATHENS • TOKYO • MILAN • MADRID
PRAGUE • WARSAW • BUDAPEST • AUCKLAND

ISBN 0-373-12415-5

THE MAGNATE'S MISTRESS

First North American Publication 2004.

www.eHarlequin.com

Printed in U.S.A.

CHAPTER ONE

THE beep-beep which signalled an incoming text message had Tara dropping her book and diving for her cellphone.

Max! It had to be Max. He was the only person who text-messaged her these days.

Arriving Mascot at 1530, she read with her heart already thudding. *QF310. Can you pick me up? Let me know.*

A glance at her bedside clock said five to twelve. If his plane was to arrive at three-thirty this afternoon, Max had to be already in the air.

She immediately texted him back.

Will be there.

She smiled wryly at the brevity and lack of sentiment in both their messages. There was no *I can't wait to see you, darling.* No *I've missed you terribly.* All very matter-of-fact.

Max was a matter-of-fact kind of man. Mostly.

Not quite so matter-of-fact in bed. A quiver rippled down Tara's spine at the image of Max in the throes of making love to her.

No. Not at all matter-of-fact on those occasions.

Tara glanced at the clock again. Nearly noon.

Not a lot of time for her to get ready, catch a train

into town, collect Max's car and drive out to the airport. She would have to hurry.

Jumping up from the bed reminded Tara of why she'd been lying back down at this late hour on a Saturday morning. A new wave of nausea rolled through her and she just made it to the bathroom in time before retching.

Darn. Why did she have to have a tummy bug today of all days? It had been almost a month since she'd seen Max, the current crisis in the travel industry having kept him on the hop overseas for ages. Hong Kong had been one of the cities worst affected. When she'd complained during his last phone call two nights ago that she'd forget what he looked like soon, Max had promised to see what he could do this weekend. He was flying to Auckland on the Friday for an important business meeting and might have time to duck over to Sydney on the weekend before returning to Hong Kong.

But Tara hadn't seriously expected anything. She never liked to get her hopes up too much. It was too depressing when she was disappointed. Still, maybe Max was finally missing her as much as she was missing him.

Which was why the last thing she needed today was to feel sick. She might only have the one night with him this time and she wanted to make the most of it. But it would be hard to enjoy his company if she felt like chucking up all the time.

A sigh reverberated through her as she flushed the toilet.

'Are you all right in there?' her mother called through the bathroom door.

'I'm fine,' Tara lied, experience warning her not to say anything. Her mother would fuss. Tara disliked being fussed over. No doubt she was only suffering from the same twenty-four-hour gastric bug which was going through Sydney's western suburbs like wildfire. Her sister's family had had it this past week, and she'd been over there last weekend for a family barbeque.

Actually, now that she'd been sick, Tara felt considerably better. A shower would make her feel even better, she reasoned, and turned on the spray.

Her arrival in the kitchen an hour later with freshly blow-dried hair, a perfectly made-up face and a new outfit on had her mother giving her a narrow-eyed once-over.

'I see his lord and master must be arriving for one of his increasingly fleeting visits,' Joyce said tartly, then went back to whatever cake she was making.

Saturday was Joyce Bond's baking day; had been for as long as Tara could remember. Such rigid routines grated on Tara's more spontaneous nature. She often wished that her mother would surprise her by doing something different on a Saturday for once. She also wished she would surprise her with a different attitude towards Max.

'Mum, please don't,' Tara said wearily, and popped

a slice of bread into the toaster. Her stomach had settled enough for her to handle some Vegemite toast, but she still wasn't feeling wonderful.

Joyce spun round from the kitchen counter to glower at her daughter. Her impossibly beautiful daughter.

Tara had inherited the best of each of her parents. She had her father's height, his lovely blond hair, clear skin, good teeth and striking green eyes. Joyce had contributed a cute nose, full lips and an even fuller bust, which looked infinitely better on Tara than it ever had on her own less tall, short-waisted body.

Joyce hadn't been surprised when one of the wealthy men who patronised the exclusive jewellery boutique where Tara worked had made a beeline for her. She wasn't surprised—or even too worried—when Tara confessed that she was no longer a virgin. Joyce had always thought it a minor miracle that a girl with Tara's looks had reached twenty-four without having slept with a man. After all, her daughter's many boyfriends must have tried to get the girl into bed.

Tara had always claimed she was waiting for Prince Charming to come along. Joyce's younger daughter was somewhat of an idealist, a full-on romantic. An avid reader, she was addicted to novels which featured wonderful heroes and happy-ever-after endings.

In the beginning, Joyce had hoped that Max Richmond *was* her daughter's Prince Charming. He had most of the attributes. Wealth. Good looks. Youth. *Relative* youth, anyway. He'd been thirty-five when they'd begun seeing each other.

But in the last twelve months Joyce had come to feel differently about her daughter's relationship with the handsome hotel magnate. It had finally become clear that Max Richmond was never going to marry his lovely young mistress.

For that was what Tara had swiftly become. Not a proper girlfriend, or a partner, as people sometimes called their loved ones these days. A *mistress*, expected to be there when he called and be silent when he left. Expected to give everything and receive nothing in return, except for the corrupting gifts rich men invariably gave to their mistresses.

Designer clothes. Jewellery. Perfume. Flowers.

A fresh bouquet of red roses was delivered every week when Max was away. But who ordered them? Joyce often wondered. The man himself, or his secretary?

If Tara had been the kind of good-time girl who could handle such a relationship, Joyce would have held her tongue. But Tara was nothing of the kind. Underneath her sophisticated and sexy-looking exterior lay a soft, sensitive soul. A good girl. When Max Richmond eventually dumped her, she was going to be shattered.

Joyce's thoughts had fired a slow-burning fury, along with her tongue.

'Don't what?' she snapped. 'Don't tell it like it is?

I'm not going to sit by silently and say nothing, Tara. I love you too much for that. You're wasting your life on that man. He will never give you what you really want. He's just using you.'

Tara refrained from reminding her mother how often she'd been told in this house that she didn't know *what* she wanted in life. Joyce had frowned over her daughter not using her arts degree to get a job in Sydney. Instead, a restless Tara had gone tripping off to Japan to teach English for two years, at the same time using the opportunity to see as much of Asia as she could. When she'd returned to Sydney eighteen months ago her mother had expected her to look for a teaching position here. Instead, she'd taken a job as a shop assistant at Whitmore Opals, till she decided what she wanted to do next. Her announcement recently that she was going back to university next year to study psychology had been met with rolling eyes, as if to say, there she goes again.

In a way, her mother was right. She didn't know what she wanted to be, career-wise, the way some people did. But she knew what she *didn't* want. She didn't want to be tied down at home with children the way Jen was. And she didn't want to bake cakes every single Saturday.

'So what *is* it that you think I really want, Mum?' she asked, rather curious to find out what secret observation her mother had made.

'Why, what most women want deep down. A home, and a family. And a husband, of course.'

Tara shook her head. Given that her mother was rising sixty, she supposed there were excuses for holding such an old-fashioned viewpoint.

But the bit about a husband was rather ironic, considering her mother's personal background. Joyce had been widowed for over twenty years, Tara's electrician father having been killed in a work accident when Tara was just three. Her mother had raised her two daughters virtually single-handed. She'd worked hard to provide for them. She'd scrimped and saved and even bought her own house. Admittedly, it was not a flash house. But it was a house. *And,* she'd never married again. In fact, there'd never been another man in her life after Tara's father.

'It may come as a surprise to you, Mum,' Tara said as she removed the popped-up toast, 'but I don't want any of that. Not yet, anyway. I'm only twenty-four. There are plenty of years ahead for me to settle down to marriage and motherhood. I like my life the way it is. I'm looking forward to going back to uni next year. Meanwhile, I have an interesting job, some good friends and a fabulous lover.'

'Whom you rarely see. As for your supposed good friends, name one you've been out with in the last six months!'

Tara couldn't.

'See what I mean?' her mother went on accusingly. 'You never go out with your old friends any more because you're compelled to keep your weekends free, in case his lord and master deigns to drop in on your life. For pity's sake, Tara, do you honestly think your jet-setting lover is spending every weekend of his alone when he doesn't come home?'

Joyce regretted the harsh words the moment she saw her daughter's face go a sickly shade of grey.

Tara gripped the kitchen counter and willed the bile in her throat to go back down. 'You don't know what you're talking about, Mum. Max would never do that.'

'Are you sure of that?' Joyce said, but more softly this time. 'He doesn't love you, Tara. Not the way you love him.'

'Yes, he does. And even if he didn't, I'd still want him.'

Oh, yes, that was one thing she *was* sure about.

'I won't give him up for anything, or anyone,' she announced fiercely, and took a savage bite of toast.

'He's going to break your heart.'

Tara's heart contracted. Would he? She couldn't imagine it. Not her Max. Not deliberately. He wasn't like that. Her mother didn't understand. Max just didn't want marriage at this time in his life. Or kids. He'd explained all that to her right from the beginning. He'd told her up front that his life was too busy for a wife and a family. Since his father had been incapacitated by a stroke, the full responsibility of running the family firm had fallen on him. Looking after a huge chain of international hotels was a massive job, especially with the present precarious state of tourism and travel. Max spent more than half his life on a plane. All he could promise her for now was the occasional weekend.

He'd given her the opportunity to tell him to get lost, *before* she got in any deeper. But of course that had been *after* he'd taken her to bed and shown her a world she'd never envisaged, a world of incredible pleasure.

How could you give up perfection, just because everything wasn't perfect?

Tara threw the rest of her toast in the bin under the sink, then straightened with a sigh. 'If you disapprove of my relationship with Max this much, Mum,' she said unhappily, 'perhaps it's time I moved out of home.'

She could well afford to rent a place of her own on her salary. Her pay as a shop assistant at Whitmore Opals was boosted by generous commission each month. She was their top salesgirl, due to her natural affinity for people and her ability to speak fluent Japanese. A lot of the shop's customers were wealthy Japanese visitors and businessmen who appreciated being served by a pretty Australian girl who spoke their language like a native.

'And go where?' her mother threw back at her. 'To your lover's penthouse? He won't like that. You're only welcome there when *he's* there.'

'You don't know that. There again, you don't know Max. How could you? You never say more than two words to him on the phone and you've never invited him here.'

'He wouldn't want to come here,' she grumbled. 'This house isn't fancy enough for a man who lives on the top floor of Sydney's plushest hotel, and whose family owns a waterfront mansion on Point Piper. *Which*, might I point out, he's not taken you to, not even over Christmas? Have you noticed that, Tara? You're not good enough to be taken home to meet his parents. You're to be kept a dirty little secret. That's what you are, Tara. A *kept* woman.'

Tara had had enough of this. 'Firstly, there is nothing dirty about my relationship with Max. We love each other and he treats me like a princess. Secondly, Max does not keep me a dirty little secret. We often go out together in public, as you very well know. You used to show your friends the photographs in the paper. Quite proudly, if I recall.'

'That was when I thought something would come of your relationship. When I thought he would marry you. But there have been no photographs in the paper lately, I've noticed. Maybe because he doesn't have time to take you out any more. But I'll bet he still has time to take you to bed!'

Tara clenched her jaw hard lest she say something she would later regret. She loved her mother dearly. And she supposed she could understand why the woman worried about her and Max. But modern life was very complicated when it came to personal relationships. Things weren't as cut and dried as they had been in Joyce's day.

Still, it was definitely time to find somewhere else

to live. Tara could not bear to have to defend herself and Max all the time. It would sour her relationship with her mother.

She could see now that she should not have come back home to live after her return from Tokyo. Her two years away had cut the apron strings and she should have left them cut. But when her mother had met her at the airport on her return, Tara didn't have the heart to dash Joyce's presumption that her daughter was back to stay with her. And frankly, it had been rather nice to come home to her old bedroom and her old things. *And* to her mother's cooking.

But that had been several months before she'd met Max and fallen head over heels in love.

Things were different now.

Still, if she moved out of home, her mother was going to be very lonely. She often said how much she enjoyed Tara's company. Tara's board money helped make life easier for Joyce as well. Her widow's pension didn't stretch all that far.

Guilt screamed in to add to Tara's distress.

Oh, dear. What was a daughter to do?

She would talk to Max about the situation, and see what he said. Max had a wonderful way of making things seem clear and straightforward. Solutions to problems were Max's stock-in-trade. As were decisions. He spent most of his life solving problems and making decisions.

Max was a very decisive man. A little inflexible,

however, Tara conceded. And opinionated. And un-forgiving.

Very unforgiving, actually.

'Look, Mum, there are reasons why Max hasn't taken me home to meet his parents,' she started explaining to her mother. 'It has nothing to do with our working class background. His own father was born working-class, but he…' Tara broke off abruptly before she revealed things told to her in strict confidence. Max would not appreciate her blurting out the skeletons in his family's closet, even to her mother. 'Let's leave all this for now,' she said with a sigh. 'I don't feel up to arguing with you over Max today.'

The moment she added those last words, Tara regretted them, for her mother's eyes instantly turned from angry to worried. Her mother was a chronic worrier when it came to matters of health.

'I *thought* I heard you being sick earlier,' Joyce said.

'It's nothing. Just a tummy bug. Probably the same thing Jen and her kids had. I'm feeling better now.'

'Are you sure that's what it is?' her mother asked, still looking concerned.

'Well, I don't think I'm dying of some dreaded disease,' Tara said. 'Truly, Mum, you have to stop looking up those health websites on the internet. You're becoming a hypochondriac.'

'I meant,' her mother bit out, 'do you think you could be pregnant?'

'Pregnant!' Tara was totally taken aback. Dear

heaven. Mothers! *Truly.* 'No, Mum, I am definitely *not* pregnant.' She'd had a period during the weeks Max had been away, which meant if she was pregnant, it had been because of an immaculate conception!

Besides, if there was one thing Tara was fanatical about, it was birth control. The last thing *she* wanted at this time in her life was a baby. Max wasn't the only one.

When they'd first become lovers, Max had said he'd use condoms. But after one broke one night last year and they'd spent an anxious two weeks, Tara had taken over the job of preventing a pregnancy. She even had her cellphone programmed so that it beeped at the same time every day, a reminder to take her pill. Six pm on the dot. She also kept a spare box of pills in Max's bathroom, in case she accidentally left hers at home.

Her mother's tendency to always expect the worst to happen in life had trained Tara to be an expert in preventative action.

'There is no sure form of contraception,' Joyce pointed out firmly. 'Except saying no.'

Tara refrained from telling her mother that saying no to Max would never be on her agenda.

'I have to get going,' she said. 'The next train for the city is due in ten minutes.'

'When will you be back?' her mother called after her as she hurried from the kitchen. 'Or don't you know?'

It hit home. That last remark. Because Tara *didn't* know. She never seemed to know these days. In that, her mother was right. Max came and went like a whirlwind, often without much information or explanation. He expected her to understand how busy he was at the moment. Which she did on the whole. *Didn't* she?

'I'll let you know, Mum,' Tara called back as she scooped up her carry-all and swept out the door. 'Bye.'

CHAPTER TWO

HER wrist-watch said three-forty as Tara slid Max's silver Mercedes into an empty parking space, then yanked the car keys out of the ignition. Ten seconds later she was hurrying across the sun-drenched car park, wishing she was wearing her joggers, instead of high-heeled slip-on white sandals. They were sexy shoes but impossible to run in. She'd found that out on the way to the station back at home.

Missing the train had put her in a right quandary.

Did she wait for the next train or catch a taxi?

A taxi from Quakers Hill to the city would cost a bomb.

Unfortunately, Joyce had instilled some of her frugal ways in both her daughters, so whilst Tara could probably have afforded the fare, she couldn't bring herself to do it. Aside from the sheer extravagance, she was saving this year to pay for next year's uni fees.

She'd momentarily contemplated using the credit card Max had given her, and which she occasionally used for clothes. But only when he was with her, and only when it was for something he insisted she buy, and which she wouldn't wear during her day-to-day life. Things like evening gowns and outrageously expensive lingerie. Things she kept in Max's penthouse for her life there.

Till now, she'd never used the card for everyday expenses. When she considered it this time, her mother's earlier words about her being a kept woman made up her mind for her. Maybe if she'd been still feeling sick, she'd have surrendered to temptation and taken a taxi, but the nausea which had been plaguing her all morning had finally disappeared. So she'd bought herself some food and sat and waited for the next train, and now she was running late.

Tara increased the speed of her stride, her stiletto heels click-clacking faster on the cement path. Her heart started to beat faster as well, a mixture of agitation and anticipation. With a bit of luck, Max's plane might not have arrived yet. She'd hate him to think she didn't care enough to be on time. Still, planes rarely seemed to land on schedule. Except when you didn't want them to, of course.

The contrariness of life.

Once inside the arrivals terminal, Tara swiftly checked the overhead information screens, groaning when she saw that Max's plane *had* landed, although only ten minutes earlier. The exit gate assigned was gate B.

Surely he could not be through Customs yet, she told herself as she hurried once more, her progress slightly hampered by having to dodge groups of people. Gate B, typically, was down the other end of the building.

Most of the men she swept past turned for a second glance, but Tara was used to that. Blondes surely did get more than their fair share of male attention, especially tall, pretty ones with long, flowing hair and even longer legs.

Tara also conceded that her new white hipsters were on the eye-poppingly tight side today. She'd been doing some comfort eating lately and had put on a couple of pounds since she'd bought them at a summer sale a fortnight ago. It was as well they were made of stretch material. Still, lord knew what the view of her was like from behind. Pretty in-your-face, no doubt.

Her braless state might have stopped traffic as well, *if* she'd been wearing a T-shirt or a singlet top.

Thankfully, she wasn't wearing either. The pink shirt she'd chosen that day did a fair job of hiding her unfettered breasts.

In her everyday life, Tara always wore a bra. But Max liked her braless. Or so he'd said one night, soon after they'd starting seeing each other. And, being anxious to please him, she'd started leaving off her bra whenever she was with him.

But as time had gone by, she'd become aware of the type of stares she'd received from other men when Max had taken her out in public.

And she hadn't liked it.

Nowadays, when she was with Max, she still left her bra off, but compromised by never wearing anything too revealing. She chose evening gowns with heavily beaded bodices, or solid linings. For dressy day wear, she stuck to dresses and covering jackets. For casual wear, she wore shirts and blouses rather than tight or clingy tops. Tara liked the idea of keeping her bared breasts for her lover only.

Her nipples tightened further at the mere thought of Max touching them.

She would have to wait for that pleasure, however, till they were alone in Max's hotel suite. Although Max seemed to like her displaying her feminine curves in public, he was not a man to make love anywhere but in total privacy. And that included kissing.

The first time he'd come home after being away, she'd thrown her arms around him in public and given him a big kiss. His expression when she finally let him come up for air had been one of agitation, and distaste. He'd explained to her later that he found it embarrassing, and could she please refrain from turning him on to that degree when he could not do anything about it?

He *had* added later that he was more than happy for her to be as provocative and as assertive as she liked in private. But once stung by what she'd seen as a rejection of her overtures—and affection—Tara now never made the first move where lovemaking was concerned. She always left it up to Max.

Not that she ever had to wait long. Behind closed doors, Max's coolly controlled façade soon dropped away to reveal a hot-blooded and often insatiable lover. His visits home might have become shorter and less frequent over the last few months—as Tara's mother had observed—but whilst he was here in Sydney, he was all Tara's. They spent most of Max's visits in bed.

Her mother would see this as conclusive evidence that she was just a sex object to Max. A kept woman. In other words, a mistress.

But her mother was not there when Max took her in his arms. She didn't see the look in his eyes; didn't feel the tenderness in his touch; or the uncontrollable trembling which racked his body whenever he made love to her.

Max *loved* her. Tara was sure of it.

His not wanting to marry her at this time in his life was a matter of timing, not lack of love. Max had never said that marriage was *never* on his agenda.

And as she'd told her mother, *she* was in no hurry to get married, anyway. What she was in a hurry for was to get to gate B, collect Max and take him back to the Regency Royale Hotel, post-haste.

Fate must have been on her side, for no sooner had she ground to a breathless halt not far from gate B than Max emerged through the customs exit, striding purposefully down the ramp, carrying his laptop in one hand and wheeling a black carry-on suitcase in the other.

Tara supposed he didn't look all that much different from dozens of other well-dressed businessmen there at the airport that day. Perhaps taller than most. More broad-shouldered. And more handsome.

But just the sight of him did things to her that she could never explain to her mother. She came alive as she was never alive when she wasn't with him. Her brain bubbled with joy and the blood fizzed in her veins.

Tara conceded not every twenty-four-year-old girl's heart would flutter madly at Max's more conservative brand of handsome, or his very conservative mode of dressing. Tara rarely saw him in anything but a suit. Today's was charcoal-grey. Single-breasted, combined with a crisp white shirt and a striped blue tie.

All very understated.

But Tara liked the air of stability and security which Max's untrendy image projected. She liked the fact that he always looked a man of substance. And she very much liked his looks.

Yet till now, she'd never really analysed him feature by feature. It had been his overall appearance, and his overall aura which had initially taken her breath away. And which had kept her captivated ever since.

But as Max made his way through gate B, his eyes having not yet connected with hers, Tara found herself studying Max's looks more objectively than usual.

Now, that was one classically handsome guy, she decided. Not a pretty boy, but not a rough diamond, either.

A masculine-looking man, Max had a large but

well-balanced face, surrounded by a thick head of dark brown hair, always cut with short back and sides, and always combed from a side-parting. His ears were nicely flat against his well-shaped head. His intelligent blue eyes were deeply set, bisected by a long, straight nose and accentuated with thick, dark brown brows. His mouth, despite its full bottom lip, had not a hint of femininity about it and invariably held an uncompromising expression.

Max was not a man who smiled a lot. Mostly, his lips remained firmly shut, his penetrating blue eyes glittering with a hardness which Tara found sexy, but which she imagined could be forbidding, especially when he was annoyed, or angry. Tara suspected he could be a formidable boss, if crossed. She'd heard him a few times over the phone when he'd been laying down the law to various employees.

But with her, he was never really annoyed, or angry. He *had* been frustrated that time when she'd kissed him in public. And exasperated when she refused to let him buy her a car. But that was it.

Tara knew that when he finally caught sight of her standing there, waiting for him, he *would* smile.

And suddenly, it was there, that slow curve to his lips, that softer gleam in his eyes, and it was all she could do not to run to him and throw herself into his arms. Instead, she stayed right where she was, smiling her joy back at him whilst he walked slowly towards her.

'For a few seconds, I thought you weren't here,' he said once they were standing face to face.

'I almost wasn't,' she confessed. 'I was running horribly late. You should have seen me a minute ago, trying to bolt across the car park in these shoes.'

He glanced down at the offending shoes, then slowly let his eyes run up her body. By the time his gaze reached her mouth, her lips had gone bone-dry.

'Are you sure it was the shoes, or those wicked white trousers? How on earth did you get them on? You must have had them sewn on.'

'They're stretchy.'

His eyes glittered in that sexy way she adored. 'Thank the lord for that. I had visions of spending half the night getting them off you. You know, you really shouldn't wear gear like that to greet me when we've been apart for nearly a month. It does terrible things to me.'

'I thought you liked me to dress sexily,' she said, piqued that he hadn't bothered to ask her why she was late. It occurred to her with a degree of shock that maybe he didn't care.

'That depends on how long I've been away. Thank goodness you're wearing a bra.'

'But I'm not.'

He stared at her chest, then up at her mouth. 'I wish you hadn't told me that,' he muttered.

'For pity's sake, Max, is there no pleasing you to-day?'

'You please me all the time,' he returned thickly,

and putting his laptop down, he actually reached out to stroke a tender hand down her cheek. If that didn't stun her, his next action did.

He kissed her, his hand sliding down and around under her hair, cupping the back of her neck whilst his mouth branded hers with purpose and passion.

The kiss must have lasted a full minute, leaving Tara weak-kneed with desire and flushed with embarrassment. For people were definitely staring at them.

'Max!' she protested huskily when his hand then slid down her shirt over her right breast.

'That's what you get for meeting me in those screw-me shoes,' he whispered.

When Tara gaped at him, Max laughed.

'You little hypocrite. You deliberately dressed to tease me today, and then you pretend to be shocked when you get the reaction you wanted. Here. Give me my car keys and take this,' he ordered and handed her the laptop. 'I want one hand free to keep you in line, you bad girl.'

Tara's cheeks continued to burn as she was ushered from the terminal with Max's hand firmly clamped to her bejeaned backside. Her head was fairly whirling with mixed messages and emotions.

In all the times she had picked Max up at the airport, he had never made her feel like this. As if sex was the *only* thing on his mind, and on hers. And whilst she was flustered by this change in behaviour—could her mother have been right about Max just using her for sex?—she was also undeniably turned on.

Neither of them said a single word till they were standing by the Mercedes and Max had put his things into the boot.

'Fifteen minutes,' Max said as he slammed the boot shut and turned to her.

'What?'

By then she was hot all over, not just her cheeks.

'Fifteen minutes,' Max repeated. 'That's how long till we're alone. I suspect it's going to be the longest fifteen minutes of my life.' His eyes ran all over her again, finally lingering on her mouth. 'If I kiss you again, I won't be able to wait. I'll ravage you in the back seat of this car and to hell with everything.'

Tara wasn't sure if she liked this beastlike Max as much as the civilised one she was used to. But she suspected that if he kissed her again, she wouldn't *care* if he ravaged her on the back seat.

In fact, she was already imagining him doing just that, and it sent her head spinning.

Just then, a couple of young fellows walked by and one of them ogled her before pursing his lips in a mock kiss. When he turned to his mate and said something, they both laughed.

Tara cringed.

'Then please don't kiss me,' she choked out.

Max, who hadn't seen this exchange, shook his head at her. 'Still playing the tease? That's a new one for you, Tara. What's happened to the sweet, naive, extremely innocent virgin I met a year ago?'

'She's been sleeping with you for a year,' she countered, stung by his inference that this change today was all hers.

His eyes darkened. 'Do I detect a degree of dissatisfaction in those words? Is that why you were late today? Because you were thinking of not coming to pick me up at all?'

'So glad that you finally cared enough to ask why I was late!' she snapped. 'For your information, I had words with my mother and then I missed my train.'

Did he look relieved? She couldn't be sure. Max was not an easy man to read.

'What was the argument about?'

'You.'

That surprised him. 'What about me?'

'Mum thinks you're just using me.'

'And what do you think?'

'I told her you loved me.'

'I do.'

Tara's heart lurched at his words. *Do you, Max? Do you, really?*

'If you truly loved me,' she pointed out agitatedly, 'then you wouldn't talk about ravaging me in the back seat of a car in a public car park.'

He seemed startled, before a thoughtful frown gathered on his high forehead. 'I see the way your mind is working, but you're wrong. And so was I. You're not a tease, or a hypocrite. You're still the incurable romantic you always were. But that's all right. That's what I love about you. Come along, then, princess. Let's get you home, where we can dive into our lovely four-poster bed and make beautiful romantic love all weekend long.'

'Do we have a whole weekend this time, Max?' Tara asked eagerly, relieved that the threat of being publicly ravaged in the back seat of Max's car had been averted.

'Unfortunately, no. I have to catch a plane back to Hong Kong around one tomorrow afternoon.

'Sorry,' he added when her face fell. 'But things there are going from bad to worse. Who knows where it will all end? Still, that's not your concern.'

'But I like to hear about your work problems,' she said truthfully, and touched his arm.

He stiffened for a second before picking up her hand and kissing her fingertips. The entire surface of Tara's skin broke out into goose-pimples.

'I haven't come home to talk about work, Tara,' he murmured. 'I've come home to relax for a night. With my beautiful girlfriend.'

Tara beamed at him. 'You called me your girlfriend.'

Max looked perplexed. 'Well, that's what you are, isn't it?'

'Yes. Yes, that's what I am. I hope,' she muttered under her breath as she turned away from him and hurried round to the passenger side.

She could feel his eyes on her as she climbed into

the car. But she didn't want to see what was in them. It was enough for now that he'd called her his girl-friend. Enough that he'd declared his love. She didn't want to see the heat in his gaze and misinterpret it. Of course he desired her, as she desired him. Of course!

But he won't ever give you what you want, Tara.

Yes, he would, she reassured herself as the car sped towards the city. Till he left for the airport tomorrow, he would give her his company, and his love, and his body. Which was all that she wanted right at this moment. His body possibly most of all.

Even now, she was thinking of the hours she would spend in bed with him, of the way she felt when he caressed and kissed her all over, when he made her melt with just a touch of his finger or a stab of his tongue. She especially liked it when he played with her endlessly, bringing her again and again to the brink of ecstasy, only to draw back at the last moment, making her wait in a state of exquisite tension till he was inside her.

Those were the best times, when they reached satisfaction together, when she held him close and she felt their hearts beating as one.

The car zoomed down into the tunnel which would take them swiftly to the city, the enveloping darkness making Tara even more aware of the man beside her. She glanced over at his strong profile, then at his hands on the wheel.

Her thighs suddenly pressed together at the thought of him taking her, her insides tightening.

When Tara sucked in sharply Max's head turned and his eyes glittered over at her. 'What are you thinking about?'

She blushed and he laughed, breaking her tension.

'Same here. But we're almost there now. It won't be long to wait.'

CHAPTER THREE

THE Regency Hotel—recently renamed the Regency Royale by Max—was situated towards the northern end of the city centre, not far from Circular Quay. Touted as one of Sydney's plushest hotels, it had a décor to suit its name. Guests could be forgiven for thinking they'd stepped back in time once they entered the reception area of the Regency, with its wood-panelled walls, velvet-covered couches and huge crystal chandeliers.

The arcade which connected the entrance of the hotel to the lobby proper was just as lavish, also resonant of England in past times, with its intricately tiled floor and stained-glass ceiling. The boutiques and bars which lined the arcade reflected a similar sense of period style and grace.

Max had once told Tara that was why he'd bought the Regency. Because of its period look.

The Royale chain specialised in hotels which weren't modern-looking in design or décor. Because modern, Max told her, always eventually dated. History and grandeur were what he looked for in a hotel.

Tara had to agree that this made sound business sense. Of all the hotels in Sydney, the Regency

Royale stood out for its style and good, old-fashioned service. But it was the look of the place which captivated guests. The day she came here for her interview at Whitmore Opals eighteen months ago, she'd spent a good while walking around the place, both amazed and admiring.

Today, however, as Max ushered her along the arcade past her place of employment, her focus was on anything but the hotel. Her thoughts were entirely on the man whose hand was clamped firmly around her elbow, and on the state of almost desperate desire he'd reduced her to.

Never, in the twelve months they'd been seeing each other, had she experienced anything quite like this. She'd always been happy for Max to make love to her. But never had she wanted him this badly.

'Afternoon, Mr Richmond,' a security guard greeted as he walked towards them.

'Afternoon, Jack,' Max replied, and actually stopped to talk to the man whilst Tara clenched her teeth in her jaw.

It was probably only a minute before they moved on but it felt like an eternity.

'Glad to see you again, Mr Richmond,' another employee chirped after a few more metres.

'Same here, Warren.'

This time Max didn't stop, thank goodness. Tara smothered a sigh of relief, even happier when Max bypassed the reception desk and headed straight for the lifts. Not that he needed to book in, for heaven's sake. But Max was a hands-on hotel owner who liked to be kept informed over the ins and outs of everything. He usually stopped by Reception for a brief chat on arrival.

In the past, Tara hadn't minded his stopping to talk to his employees. She'd always admired the way Max knew every employee by their first name, from the valet-parking attendants to the managers.

Today, however, she was extremely irritated by the delays. Which wasn't like her at all.

The alcove which housed the lifts was not empty. A man in his forties, and presumably his wife, were standing there, waiting for a lift. They didn't look like tourists. Or members of Sydney's élite. Their clothes and faces betrayed them as working-class Australians, perhaps staying here in Sydney's flashest hotel for some special event, or occasion.

'I will never stay in this hotel again,' the man grumbled. 'I'd go somewhere right now if it didn't mean losing my deposit. I couldn't believe that girl, insisting that I hadn't booked a harbour-view room. As if I would bring you here for our silver anniversary and not get the very best room I could afford.'

'It doesn't matter, Tom,' the wife placated. 'I'm sure all the rooms here are lovely.'

'That's not the point. It's the principle of the thing. And that girl behind the desk was quite rude, I thought.'

'Not really,' the woman said with a nervous glance

towards Max and Tara. 'It was just a mix-up. These things happen. Let's try not to let it spoil our night.'

Tara smothered a groan when she felt Max's fingertips tighten around her elbow. She knew, as she glanced up at his tightly drawn face, that he was going to do something about this situation.

'Excuse me, sir,' he said, just as the lift doors opened. 'But I couldn't help overhearing. I'm Max Richmond, the owner of this hotel. If you'll allow me, I'd like to accompany you back to Reception, where I will sort this out to your satisfaction.'

'Max,' Tara whispered urgently.

'You go on, darling,' he said. 'I'll be up as quick as I can. Slip into something more comfortable,' he murmured as he pecked her on the cheek.

Tara stared after him as he led the awestruck couple away, struggling to contain her bitter disappointment and understand that of course, he couldn't have done anything else. Not her Max. Hadn't she tried to tell her mother what a good man he was?

But did he have to be good right at this moment? She would have much preferred him to be bad. *Very* bad.

Again, Tara was amazed by the intensity of her craving, her sudden wish for Max to make love to her not quite so tenderly as he usually did. Maybe Max had been right after all. Maybe she *had* dressed as she had today to tease and arouse him. Yet her clothes weren't all that different from what she usually wore. This change seemed to be coming from inside her.

Now that she came to think of it, she felt more aware of her body than usual today. Her breasts. Her nipples. Her belly. She craved to have them stroked, and licked, and kissed. She craved…oh, she wasn't sure what she craved. She just craved.

Agitated, Tara fished her keycard out of her bag and hurried into the lift before anyone else could come along. She wanted to be alone with her frustrations, and her bewilderment.

But she wasn't alone in the lift. She had company. Herself, in the reflection she made in the mirrored section of the walls. Was that her, the creature looking back at her with dilated green eyes and flushed cheeks?

Yes. That was her. Tara, the suddenly sex-mad tart.

Shaking her head at herself, Tara dropped her gaze to the floor for the ride up, determined not to look up into those knowing mirrors till the lift doors opened.

The mirrors were actually a new addition, Max having had the lifts recently renovated in keeping with the rest of the hotel. The floor she was staring down at was now covered in thick red carpet which ran up the walls to waist height, at which point the mirrors took over.

Tara knew without glancing up that the ceiling overhead shone like gold. Probably not in real gold but the effect was the same. Recessed lighting was the only visible concession to the twenty-first century, along with the tiny and very discreet cameras situated in the corners.

Tight security was a must in the Regency Royale, its guest list ranging from pop stars to presidents, with the occasional prince thrown in for good measure. There was even a heliport on top of the building so that these more esteemed guests could arrive and leave with less drama and more safety. Nevertheless, Max only allowed a few helicopter movements each week, partly because of local-authority restrictions but mostly because he couldn't stand the noise himself. His penthouse apartment occupied the floor just below the heliport.

Everything was deathly quiet, however, when Tara emerged from the lift into the spacious lobby which led to the penthouse door. She used another passkey to let herself inside, where it was almost as quiet, just a small humming sound from the air-conditioning which kept all the rooms at a steady twenty-four degrees Celsius, regardless of the temperature outside.

The perfect temperature for lovers and lovemaking, came the immediate thought. For being naked and walking around naked.

This last thought startled Tara. Because that was one thing she never did. Walked around naked. The idea was theoretically exciting, but the reality made her cringe. She would feel embarrassed, and awkward.

Or would she?

Tara knew she looked good in the buff. Certainly better than most girls, though she couldn't claim this was due to any hard work on her part. Mother nature had just been kind to her. Tara suspected Max wouldn't have minded if she'd been a little less shy. He was always asking her to join him in the shower and she always refused.

Maybe this weekend might be a good place to try to overcome that particular hang-up. She doubted she would ever feel as wicked, or as driven, as she did at this moment. She could not wait to get her hands on Max. The thought of washing him all over in the shower was not unattractive, just a bit daunting.

A shudder ran through her. She would think about that later. There were other things she had to do first, such as whip around and turn some lamps on.

Max loved lamp-light, and whilst it was still bright and sunny outside—the sun wouldn't set for hours— the inside of Max's penthouse always required some lighting. Mostly this was due to the wraparound terraces and the wide eaves. On top of that, the décor of the penthouse was very much in keeping with the décor of the hotel, which meant it wasn't madly modern like some penthouses, with great open-plan living areas and huge plate-glass windows.

The décor was still period, with wallpapered walls and rich carpets on the floors. French doors lead out onto the balconies and heavy silk curtains draped over the windows. The furniture was all antique. Warm woods covered in velvet or brocade in rich colours. It was like an Edwardian English mansion set up in the sky. As big as a mansion too, with formal lounge and dining rooms, four bedrooms, three bathrooms, a study, a library, a billiard room, along with a large kitchen, laundry and utility rooms.

Everything was exquisite and *very* expensive.

Tara hadn't realised the size or extravagance of the place on the first night she'd spent with Max. She'd been overwhelmed by the events and the experience, rather than her surroundings. But the following morning, she'd soon been confronted by the extreme wealth of the man who'd just become her first lover. Initially, she'd been dumbstruck, then totally convinced that he would only want a girl like her for a one-night stand.

But Max had reassured her for the rest of that incredible weekend that a casual encounter was not what he wanted from her at all. Tara recalled thinking at the time that she had found nothing casual in letting him take her virginity less than three hours after she'd first set eyes on him. If she hadn't known she'd fallen instantly and deeply in love with the man, she would have been disgusted with herself.

Naturally, she'd been thrilled that he found her as special as she found him, and here she was, one year later, with her own private key, getting things ready for her man in the way that women in love had done so for centuries. If it fleetingly crossed Tara's mind that her role in her lover's life *was* more like a mistress than a real girlfriend, she dismissed it with the added thought that it wouldn't always be like this. One day, things would change. Max would have more time for her. Till then, she aimed to enjoy the time with him she did have and that part of him which was solely hers.

At least, she *hoped* it was solely hers.

Yes, of course it was. Her mother was wrong about that, as she was wrong about Max all round. The man who was at this moment doing nice things for that couple downstairs was not the kind of man to be unfaithful, or a callous user. She really had to stop letting her mother undermine her faith in Max, or spoil what promised to be a very exciting night.

With a defiant toss of her head, Tara turned and hurried down the plushly carpeted corridor which led to Max's personal quarters, fiercely aware that the last few minutes away from Max's rousing presence hadn't dampened her desires in the slightest. In fact, having sex with Max was all she could think about at that moment, which was not her usual priority when Max came home these days. Mostly, she just wanted to spend time with the man she loved. His lovemaking, though wonderful, was more of a bonus than the be-all and end-all.

Today, it was not only top priority, but close to becoming an emergency!

It was Max's fault, she decided as she swept into the bedroom and starting fumbling with the tiny pearl buttons of her pink shirt. The way he'd looked at her at the airport. The things he'd said about her clothes. That kiss, and then his threat to ravage her on the back seat of the car.

Tara finally stripped off her blouse then kicked off her shoes.

'My screw-me shoes,' she said with a wicked little laugh as she bent to pick them up, carrying the shirt and the shoes into the adjoining dressing room, where she'd put her bag earlier on. There, she stripped off her jeans and undies, stuffing them into the bag's side-pocket for later washing. The shirt she hung up in her section of the walk-in wardrobe. The shoes she put into the special shoe rack before running her eyes along the clothes she kept at Max's place, looking for something more comfortable to slip into.

Her mother's *kept*-woman tag flashed into her mind at the sight of so many designer evening gowns, all paid for by Max, each worn to one of the many swanky dos Max had taken her to during the first few months of their relationship. Dinner parties at the homes of top politicians. Gala openings at the opera house. Art exhibitions. Balls. The races.

You name it, she'd been there on Max's arm.

Actually, she *had* objected the first time he'd suggested buying her a designer dress. But he'd swept aside her possibly feeble protest with what had seemed like acceptable reasoning.

He could well afford it, he'd pronounced. But possibly his most persuasive argument of all was that it gave him great pleasure to see his gorgeous girlfriend in clothes befitting her beauty.

How could she possibly say no?

The lingerie, Tara realised as her eyes shifted further along the rack, had been more recent gifts, brought home from Max's more frequent trips overseas. She had negligee sets from Paris, London, Rome, New York.

These were all she seemed to wear for him these days, now that she came to think of it. Max hadn't taken her outside the door of this penthouse for some time. No doubt he wouldn't this evening either.

'Good!' she pronounced aloud with a dizzying rush of excitement, and pulled out a green satin wrap which she knew complemented her fair colouring and green eyes. The matching nightgown she left on the hanger. No point in wearing *too* much.

Tossing the wrap over her arm, she headed for the bathroom and was about to have a quick shower before Max arrived when she remembered she hadn't put her pills and her mobile phone on the bedside chest as she usually did. Dashing back to the dressing room, she retrieved the items from her bag and bolted into the bedroom to do just that. Then she stopped to quickly turn the bedclothes back before glancing around to see that everything was ready for a romantic interlude.

Not that Max's bedroom needed anything to enhance its already romantic décor. Everything about it was rich and sensual. The soft gold carpet was extra thick and the gold-embossed cream wallpaper extra rich, both perfect foils for the dark mahogany wood used in all the elegant furniture. The four-poster bed. The bedside chests. The dressing table and matching stool. The cheval mirror that stood in one corner and the wingbacked chairs that occupied the other corners.

The soft furnishings were rich and sensual-looking as well, all made in a satin-backed brocade which carried a gold fleur-de-lis design over an olive-green background. A huge crystal and brass chandelier hung from the centre of the ceiling, but there were also several dainty crystal wall lights dotted around the room.

Tara loved it when it was dark and all the lights were turned off except those. The room took on a magical glow which was so romantic. Much better than the bedside lamps which she thought threw too much light onto the bed. And them.

Of course, the pièce de résistance in Max's bedroom was the four-poster bed. Huge, it was, with great carved posts and bedhead. The canopy above was made of the same material as all the other soft furnishings, draped around the edges and trimmed with a gold fringe. There were side-curtains, which theoretically could be drawn to surround the bed, but were always kept pulled back and secured to the bedposts with gold tasselled cords.

Tara ran her fingers idly through one of the tassels and wondered what it would be like to be in bed with Max with the curtains drawn.

'What are you thinking now?'

'Oh!' Tara gasped, whirling to find Max standing in the doorway of the bedroom, staring at her with coldly glittering eyes.

'I... I didn't hear you come in,' she babbled, her heart pounding madly as she tried to cover herself with her hands.

With a sigh Max stalked into the room, his face now showing exasperation. 'Don't you think we've gone past that, Tara? I mean, I do know what you look like naked. Surely you must know that I'd *like* it if you walked around in front of me nude,' he finished as he took off his jacket and threw it onto the nearest chair.

She just stared at him, her heartbeat almost in suspension. But her mind was racing. Yes, yes, it was saying. I'd like to do that, too. Truly. I just can't seem to find the courage.

'And there I was,' he muttered as he yanked his tie off, 'thinking today that you might have finally decided you wanted more than for me to make love to you under the covers with the lights turned down.

'It's all right,' he added a bit wearily when she remained frozen and tongue-tied. 'I understand. You're shy. Though heaven knows why. You have the most beautiful body God ever gave to a woman. And you're passionate enough, between the sheets.'

Turning away from her, he tossed the tie on top of the jacket then started undoing the buttons on his shirt.

'Go and put something on,' he bit out, not looking at her. 'If you must.'

Tara dashed into the bathroom and shakily pulled on the green wrap, hating herself for feeling relieved.

When she finally returned to the bedroom, Max was sitting on the foot of the bed, taking off his shoes and socks. His shirt was hanging open, but he hadn't taken it off.

Tara's heart sank. Did he think she was *that* modest? She *loved* his chest, with its broad shoulders, wonderfully toned muscles and smattering of curls.

'Did…did you fix up things for those people?' she asked somewhat sheepishly.

'Naturally,' he replied without looking up at her. 'I had them moved into one of the honeymoon suites, on the house. And I told them they could have a free harbour-view room for their anniversary next year.'

'Oh, Max, that was generous of you. And very smart. That man would have bad-mouthed the hotel for years, you know. To anyone who would listen. Now he'll say nothing but good things. People love getting something for free. I know I do. I can never resist those buy-one, get one-free promotions.'

'Really?' He finally looked up, but his clouded eyes indicated that he was suddenly off in another world. Max did that sometimes. Tara knew better than to ask him what he was thinking about. Whenever she did, he always said 'nothing important'.

'So which honeymoon suite are they in?' she asked instead. The hotel was famous for its four themed honeymoon suites, which Tara knew cost a bomb to stay in. Bookings showed that the Arabian Nights suite was the most popular, followed by the Naughty

Nautical suite, the French Bordello suite and, lastly, the Tropical Paradise suite.

'What? Oh, there was only the one available tonight. The French Bordello. Mr Travis seemed tickled pink. Can't say the same for Mrs Travis. She seemed a little nervous. Maybe she's on the shy side. Like you.'

'I'm not all that shy,' Tara dared to say at last.

Max darted her a dry look.

'All right, I am, a bit,' she went on, swallowing when he stood up and started undoing his trouser belt.

The prospect of watching him strip down to total nakedness before he'd even kissed her was definitely daunting. But at the same time she wanted him to, wanted him to do what she wasn't bold enough to do, wanted him to force her to stop being so silly.

'Don't panic,' he said drily and, whipping out his belt, deposited it with his other clothes. 'I won't take anything more off. I'm going to have a shower, and when I come out I'll be wearing my bathrobe. Meantime, why don't you order us something from Room Service? I don't know about you but I'm starving. I nodded off on the plane so I didn't get to eat anything. I've made us a booking for dinner at eight but that's hours away.'

'We're going out to dinner?' Tara said, taken aback.

'I've only booked the restaurant here in the hotel. Is that all right with you?'

'Oh, yes. I love going to dinner with you there. It's

just that…well, the last couple of times you've come home, we've eaten in.'

'Yes, I know. And I'm sorry. That was selfish of me. But, as I said earlier, you're a different girl between the sheets, so I try to keep you there as long as possible.'

She blushed. 'Don't make fun of me, Max.'

He groaned and walked round to draw her into his arms. 'I'm not making fun of you, princess. I would never do that. You're you and I love you just the way you are.'

'Kiss me, Max,' she said quite fiercely.

His eyes searched hers. 'I don't think that's a good idea. Not yet.'

'But I can't wait any longer!'

'*You* can't wait. Hell, Tara, what is it with you today? Are you punishing me for neglecting you lately?'

'I just want you to kiss me. No, I *need* you to kiss me.'

With a groan, he kissed her. Then he kissed her some more, till her knees went to water and she was clinging to him for dear life. When he swept her up and dropped her less than gently onto the bed, Tara made no protest. Neither did she turn her eyes away whilst he started ripping off the rest of his clothes.

She wanted to look. Wanted to see him wanting her.

Her breath caught at the extent of his desire.

He loomed over her, tugging the sash of her robe

undone, throwing the sides back to bare her body to his blazing eyes.

For what felt like an eternity, he drank her in, leaving her breathless and blushing. Then, with a few more savage yanks, the satin robe joined his clothes on the floor.

There was no tender foreplay. No gentle kisses all over. Just immediate sex. Rough and raw. Maybe not quite ravagement but close to.

And oh, how she thrilled to the primitive urgency of his passion. And to her own.

She splintered apart in no time, rocked by the force of her orgasm, overwhelmed by the experience, and by a degree of emotional confusion.

As the last spasm died away, a huge wave of exhaustion flooded Tara's body, her limbs growing as heavy as her eyelids. She could not keep them open. She could not stay awake. With a sigh, she sank into the abyss of sleep.

CHAPTER FOUR

MAX stared down at her with a stunned look on his face.

Asleep! She'd fallen asleep!

He shook his head in utter bewilderment. Tara never fell asleep afterwards.

On top of that, she'd actually *enjoyed* his making love to her like that! Hell, no, she'd *exulted* in it! She'd dragged him over the edge with her in record time. And now she was out like a light, more peaceful than he'd ever seen her.

Relief swamped him at the realisation he didn't have to feel *too* much remorse over losing control and being less than the careful, considerate, patient lover he'd come to believe Tara wanted, and needed. *Not* losing control when he was around her this past year had been a terrible battle between the lust she evoked in him, and the love.

Max thought he'd done pretty well…until today.

If only she hadn't met him looking delicious in those skin-tight jeans and those sexy shoes. If only she hadn't told him she wasn't wearing a bra. If only he hadn't kissed her then and there.

His relationship with Tara was full of 'if only's, the main one being if only he hadn't stopped to look in the window of Whitmore Opals that Friday night, and spotted her inside.

It had been lust at first sight. When she'd agreed to have drinks with him less than ten minutes after his going in and introducing himself, he'd been sure he was in for a wild night with a woman of the world. With his impossible workload and repeated overseas trips, Max's sex life had been reduced to the occasional one-nighter with women who knew the score, and Tara seemed just the ticket to ride.

But the reality had proven so different. Her telling him shakily that she was a virgin even before he'd got her bra off had certainly put the brakes on the type of activities he'd been planning. Max had been shocked, but also entranced. Who would have believed it?

Fortunately, finding out before he'd gone too far gave him the opportunity to slow things down and make sure her first experience was pleasurable and not painful. He'd taken her to bed and really taken his time with her.

Looking back, making love to her at all had probably been a mistake. He should have cut and run. But he hadn't; that very first time had made him swiftly decide that one night with Tara would not be enough. He'd kept her in his bed all weekend, making love to her as he hadn't made love to a female in years. Sweetly. Tenderly. And totally selflessly.

Unfortunately, this was what Tara came to expect from him every time. Max soon realised he was dealing with a girl whose appearance belied her real nature. Underneath the sexy-looking blonde surface, the long legs and fabulous boobs, lay a naively romantic girl.

In *some* ways, Tara could be surprisingly mature. She was well-educated, well-read and well-travelled. And she certainly had a way with people, exuding a charm and social grace far beyond her years.

But when it came to sex she was like a hothouse flower, gorgeous to look at but incredibly soft and fragile.

Or so he'd thought, up till now.

Max sat back on his haunches and stared down at her beautiful but unconscious body, lying in shameless abandonment in front of his eyes.

If only she would lie like that for him when she was awake…

Max almost laughed at this new 'if only'.

But maybe she would in the near future, came the exciting thought. She'd said she wasn't totally shy and maybe she wasn't. Maybe she just lacked the confidence to do what she really wanted to do. All she needed was some masterful persuasion at the right time, and a whole new world would open for her.

Up till this moment, Max had reluctantly accepted that Tara didn't seem the raunchy type of girl. He'd reasoned it was worth sacrificing some more exotic experiences to feel what Tara could make him feel, what she'd made him feel from their very first night together.

But tonight had shown him that maybe, they could share more erotic lovemaking together in future.

Max became aroused just thinking of the things he'd like to do with her, and her with him. Not a good idea when it looked as if she would be asleep for some time. A shower was definitely called for. A cold one.

Wincing at his discomfort, he climbed off the bed and carefully eased the bedclothes from underneath Tara's luscious derriere, rolling her gently onto the bottom sheet before pulling the other one up to her shoulders. She stirred but didn't wake, though the sheet did slip down to reveal one of her incredible breasts.

Max bent and pressed his lips softly to the exposed nipple before whirling away and heading straight for the bathroom.

CHAPTER FIVE

'WHAT?'

The startled word shot from Tara's lips as she sat bolt upright in bed. She blinked, then glanced somewhat glazedly around before realising what had woken her so abruptly.

It was the alarm on her mobile phone, telling her it was six o'clock, reminding her it was time to take her pill.

With a groan, she leant over and picked up the small pink handset, pressing the button which turned off the alarm. The sudden silence in the room highlighted Max's absence. She wondered where he was, then wished she hadn't. She didn't want to think about Max at that moment.

Tara retrieved her packet of pills from the bedside chest, popped today's pill through the foil then swallowed it promptly without bothering about getting any water. The doctor had warned her that you had to take the mini Pill around the same time every day or risk getting pregnant. Tara didn't take hers *around* the same time. She took it at *exactly* the same time every day.

That done, she threw back the sheet and—after checking that Max wasn't lurking in the doorway watching her—Tara rose to her feet. She winced at the wetness between her legs.

Impossible to pretend any longer that she didn't remember what had happened before she fell asleep.

Why she was even trying to forget suddenly annoyed her. She hadn't done anything to be ashamed of. Neither had Max, for that matter.

So he'd made love to her more forcefully than usual. So what? He'd delivered exactly what she'd been subconsciously wanting since he'd threatened to ravage her at the airport. And how she'd loved it!

Tara quivered all over at the memory. Had she ever experienced anything with Max quite so powerful before? She didn't think so.

The sight of her green wrap lying tidily across the foot of the bed brought a frown to her forehead. Max must have picked it up off the floor whilst she was asleep. His own clothes as well. They were now draped over one of the chairs.

He hadn't dressed again, she realised with a tightening of her stomach. He was somewhere in the penthouse, probably wearing nothing but his favourite bathrobe. Tara hurried into the bathroom to check, and yes, his bathrobe was missing from where it usually hung on the back of the bathroom door. And his towels were still damp. Obviously, he'd showered whilst she'd been asleep.

Swallowing, Tara hung her wrap up on the empty hook behind the door, wound her hair into a knot on top of her head, then stepped into the spacious, marble-lined shower cubicle.

She wasn't yet sure what she was going to do after she'd showered. All she knew was that her body was already rebuilding a head of steam far hotter than the water which was currently cascading over her body.

She didn't spend much time in the shower. Just long enough to ensure that she was freshly washed and nicely perfumed. She was careful not to wet her hair. She didn't want to present herself to Max like some bedraggled kitten come in from a storm. Her hair was not at its best when wet. And she wanted to look her *very* best.

No, Tara amended mentally as she towelled herself down then slipped her arms into the silky wrap. She didn't want to look her best, but her sexiest. She wanted to tempt Max into stopping doing whatever he was doing and take her back to bed. Right now.

For a second she almost left the wrap hanging open, but in the end decided that was tacky. So she tied it just as tightly as usual. Actually, even a bit tighter, so that her small waist was emphasised, as well as the rest of her curvy figure.

Swallowing, Tara took one final glance in the huge mirror which stretched along above the double vanity basins. On another day, at another time, she would have taken the time to make her face up all over again. There was little of her pink lipstick left, and her mascara had smudged all around her eyes. But she rather liked her slightly dishevelled look. She even liked the way her hair was up. Roughly, with some escaping strands hanging around her face. She looked like a woman who'd just come from her lover's bed. She looked…wanton.

Spinning on her bare heels, Tara headed for the bedroom door.

The hallway that led from the master bedroom to the main body of the penthouse seemed to go on forever. By the time she reached the main living room, she wasn't sure if she was terrified or over-excited. Her heart was going like a jack-hammer and her mouth was drier than the Simpson Desert.

But Max was not there.

Disappointment rather than relief showed her that nerves were not the most dominating force in her body at that moment. Desire was much stronger.

Whirling, she hurried down the hallway which led to Max's den, his favourite area of the penthouse when he was up and about. It was actually two rooms, connected by concertina doors which were always kept open. The first room you entered was a study-cum-library, a very masculine room with no windows, book-lined walls, a desk in one corner and several oversized, leather-studded chairs in which to sit and read. The next room was the billiard room, which had a huge, green-felted billiard table, a pub-like bar in one corner, complete with stools, and lots of French doors which opened onto the balcony.

Max was an excellent snooker player and had tried to teach Tara in their early days together, when they had time for more than bed. But she was never much good and they hadn't played in ages.

Tara wasn't about to suggest a game today. She had other games in mind, a thought which both shocked and stirred her. She'd never thought of making love as a game before.

Her hand shook as it reached for the brass door knob but no way was she going to back out now. But she didn't barge straight in. Tara had been brought up with better manners than that. She tapped on the door before she opened it, then popped her head inside.

Max, she swiftly saw, was sitting in his favourite chair, bathed in a circle of soft light from the lamp which stood behind the chair. Yes, he was wearing the white towelling bathrobe, she noted. And yes, nothing else, not even on his feet.

But he wasn't exactly sitting around, impatiently waiting for her to wake up so that he could make love to her again. He was working. *And* drinking. His laptop was open and balanced across his thighs, he was sipping a very large Scotch and chatting to someone on the phone at the same time.

Max was one of those rare men who could actually do more than one thing at a time.

'Ah, there you are,' she said, containing her irritation with difficulty.

Instead of asking him if it was all right if she interrupted him, as she usually would have, Tara walked straight in and shut the door behind her.

He was taken aback, she could see. But that was just too bad. This was *her* time with him, no one else's.

When he put up his hand towards her in a stopping gesture and kept on talking—something about a website—rebellion overcame Tara's usually automatic tendency to obey him. Slowly, she moved towards him across the expanse of dark green carpet, her hips swaying seductively, her breasts moving underneath the wrap. The act of walking parted the silky material around her knees, giving tantalising glimpses of her bare legs.

One of his brows arched as he eyed her up and down. 'I'll have to speak to you later, Pierce,' he said into the phone. 'Something's just come up.'

'*Much* later,' Tara said as he clicked off the call. Pierce was only Max's PA, after all. He could wait.

Max smiled an odd smile before dropping his eyes back to the laptop screen. 'I have something I have to finish up here first, Tara,' he said without looking up at her again. 'Why don't you toddle off back to bed and I'll join you there as soon as I can?'

Pique fired her tongue before she could think better of it. 'What if I don't want to go back to bed? What if I want to stay here? What if I want you to stop working right here and now?'

Slowly, his eyes rose. Hard and glittering, they were, just as she liked them. He sipped some more of his drink whilst he studied her over the rim of the glass.

His gaze was knowing. He was mentally stripping her, making her face flush and her nipples tighten.

'*Make* me,' he said at last, his voice soft and low and dark.

His challenging words sent a bolt of electricity zig-zagging through her, firing her blood *and* her resolve not to weaken. Because she knew what he wanted. He wanted to see her, *all* of her. Not lying in a bed, but standing upright, in front of him. Facing him.

Her heartbeat quickened whilst her hands went to the sash on her wrap. She might have fumbled if the knot had been difficult, but she only had to tug the ends of the ties to make the bow unravel. In a split-second, the sides of the wrap fell apart.

But he showed no reaction whatsoever, just went back to sipping his drink.

Shock at his low level of interest held her frozen, and finally, his eyes dropped back to the screen in his lap.

'Go back to bed, Tara,' he said. 'Clearly, you're not cut out for the role of seductress just yet.'

Stung, she stripped the robe off and dropped it to the floor. When he still didn't pay her any attention, she went right up to him and banged the lid of the laptop down.

'*Look* at me,' she hissed.

He looked at her, his narrow-eyed gaze now travelling with exquisitely exciting slowness over every inch of her nakedness.

'Very nice,' he murmured. 'But it's nothing I haven't seen before.'

'You might see something new,' she threw at him, 'if you put that drink down. And that infernal computer.'

He closed the laptop and placed it beside the chair, but kept the drink. He looked her over again as he leant back into the chair and took another mouthful of whisky.

Now fear did return. The fear of making a fool of herself.

'I'm waiting,' he said, and finally placed the near-empty glass on the small round side-table next to the chair.

Tara swallowed.

'Come, come, Tara. This is *your* show. I'm curious to see how far you'll go before you turn tail and run. I'm not going to help you one little bit.'

Tara gaped at him as the realisation struck that he didn't just want her to parade herself in front of him. He wanted *her* to make love to *him*.

If he'd issued this type of challenge on any other day before today, she probably *would* have turned tail and run. But today was a different day in more ways than one. Today, a new and exciting dimension had entered their relationship and she refused to retreat from it.

Don't think, she told herself as she stepped forward to stand between his stretched-out legs. Just do what he thinks you don't dare to do.

She heard his sharp intake of breath when she knelt down and reached for the sash on his robe.

Don't look up at his face, she warned herself shakily.

She didn't want to see any undermining shock, or surprise, in his eyes. He'd told her once he didn't mind how provocative or assertive she was in private. Well, he was just about to get a dose of provocative assertiveness, even if she was quaking inside.

The sash on his robe was as easy to undo as her own, being only looped over. Pushing the sides of the robe back was not so easy, because she knew what would confront her when she did so.

Her eyes widened at the sight of him.

So his apparent uninterest had all been a lie! He was already aroused. Fiercely so.

Tara resisted the urge to close her eyes and put her mind elsewhere. Her days of cowardice were over. She *would* look at him there, and touch him there, and kiss him there.

Yet oddly, once she started stroking the velvety length of him, once she felt Max quiver and grow even harder beneath her hands, any reluctance or revulsion melted away. Tara found herself consumed by the intense desire to make the beast emerge in him again, to drive him wild with pleasure and need, to love him as she had never loved him before.

Max could not believe it when she took him into her mouth, making the blood roar through his veins, his flesh expand even further, threatening to make him lose all control.

Surely she would not want that. Surely not!

Max groaned his worry that he might not be able to stop himself. Then groaned again when her head lifted, showing him that he had wanted her to continue more than anything he had wanted in a long time.

But any disappointment was swiftly allayed by her crawling up onto the chair onto his lap. She was even at that moment straddling his tautly held thighs, her knees fitting into the far corners of the chair.

He gasped when she took him in her hands again and directed him up into her body. Her hot, wet, delicious body. She sank downwards and suddenly he was there, totally inside her. Her face lifted and their eyes met, hers dilated, his stunned.

'Max,' was all she said before she bent down to kiss his mouth, her hands cupping his face, her tongue sliding deep into his mouth.

How often had he hoped for a Tara like this?

Then she began to ride him. Slowly at first, but then with more passion. The wilder rise and fall of her hips wrenched her mouth away from his. Her hands fell to his shoulders to steady herself, her fingernails biting into his flesh till suddenly her back arched, her flesh gripping his like a vice.

'Oooh,' she cried out.

The power of her climax was mind-blowing. He exploded in erotic response, the pleasure blinding as, all the while, she kept moving upon him, rocking back and forth, her eyes shut, her breathing ragged.

Afterwards, she sank down against his chest, her head nestling into the base of his throat. His arms encircled her back and he held her like that for quite a while, both of them silent and content.

But inevitably, the significance of what had just happened came home to him. His gorgeous Tara had finally abandoned her inhibitions.

Suddenly, he wanted her in every way a man and a woman could make love.

Tara sat up straight, her startled eyes searching his.

'Too soon?' he said, his hands sliding down her back to cup her bottom.

She shook her head.

He kept on caressing her bottom, and soon her lips fell apart on a sensual sigh of surrender. Max had never felt such love for her. Or such desire.

He was glad that their dinner reservation wasn't till eight o'clock. He had plans for the hour and a half till then, and none of them had anything to do with going back to bed.

CHAPTER SIX

'THAT gold colour looks fabulous on you,' Max said as they waited for the lift to take them down to the restaurant. 'So does the dress. I'm glad you took my suggestion to wear it tonight.'

Tara almost laughed. *Suggestion!* He hadn't suggested. He'd insisted.

The dress was a cheong-san, brought home by Max after an earlier trip to Hong Kong. Made in gold satin, it might have looked demure with its knee-length hem and high Chinese collar, except for the fact it was skin-tight, with slits up the sides which exposed a good deal of thigh. It was an extremely sensual garment.

Not that Tara needed help in feeling sensual at that moment. The last couple of hours had left all her senses heightened and her body humming. She'd certainly aroused the beast in Max with her provocative behaviour, along with another couple of Maxes. Max, the insatiable. And Max, the rather ruthless.

She shivered at the memory of the interlude on the billiard table.

Tara had briefly thought of sex as a game before going into Max's den. She hadn't realised at the time that Max was far ahead of her in the playing of erotic games, making her now wonder how many other women he'd entertained in the past in such a fashion.

At least, she *hoped* they'd been in the past.

A long and more objective look at Max—so resplendent tonight in black tie—confirmed what Tara had always subconsciously known. That women would throw themselves at him in droves. *She* had, hadn't she?

'Max,' she said with sudden worry in her voice and in her eyes.

'What, my darling?'

When he took her hand and raised it to his lips, she looked deep into *his* eyes.

'Have you ever been unfaithful to me?'

'Never,' he returned, so swiftly and so strongly that she had to believe him.

And yet…

'Why do you ask?' he went on, clearly perturbed by her question.

'I can see by tonight,' she said carefully, 'that I haven't exactly…satisfied you these past twelve months.'

'That's not true, Tara. I've been very happy with you,' he claimed.

A flicker in his eyes, however, showed otherwise.

'I don't believe you, Max. Tell me the truth.'

'Look, I admit there have been moments when I wished you were more comfortable with your body, and your sexuality. But I was not discontented. I love *you*, Tara, not just making love to you. Still, I'm glad you've finally realised that sex can be enjoyed in lots of different ways. It doesn't always have to be slow and serious. It can be fast and furious. Or it can just be fun. You had fun tonight, didn't you?'

Fun. Had it been fun? It had certainly been exciting, and compelling.

'I…I guess so.'

His smile was wry. 'Come, now, Tara. You loved it. All of it. Don't deny it.'

'I guess I'm just not used to being so wicked.'

'Wicked!' Max exclaimed, laughing. 'We weren't wicked. A little naughty perhaps. But not wicked. I could show you wicked later tonight, if you'd like.'

'What…what do you mean? Doing what?'

'I've always wanted to put those cords around my bed to far better use than tying back the curtains.'

Tara tried to feel scandalised. Instead, curiosity claimed her. What would it feel like for Max to tie her to the bed, to render her incapable of stopping him from looking at her all over, and touching her all over?

Just thinking about it gave her a hint as to what it would actually feel like. *Wicked.*

Heat filled her face. And the rest of her.

'I can see that's a bit of a leap for you,' Max said wryly. 'Forget I mentioned it.'

But how *could* she forget? He'd put the image into her mind. She would never be able to look at that bed now without thinking of herself bound to the bed-posts!

The lift doors opened. When she stood there, still in a daze, Max took her hand and pulled her into the lift.

'Come along, princess, stop the daydreaming. We have to go down and eat. We're already a quarter of an hour late, courtesy of your keeping me in the shower longer than I intended.'

'*Me* keeping *you* in the shower!' she gasped. 'You liar! It was *you*. You wouldn't let me get out till I…till I…'

'Till you'd finished what you started. Yes, I know. Sorry. You're right. I got a bit carried away. But I didn't hear you objecting.'

'I could hardly speak at the time,' she countered with a defiant glower.

He laughed. 'That's the girl. Give it back to me. That's what I want from you always, Tara. Lots of fire and spirit. I'm never at my best around yes people.'

'That's rubbish, Max, and you know it. You love yes people. I hear you on the phone all the time, giving orders and expecting to be instantly obeyed. You like being the boss, in the bedroom as well as everywhere else! You expect all your lackeys to do exactly what they're told, when they're told.'

'Aah, yes, but you're not one of my lackeys.'

'I'm not so sure,' she snapped. 'Isn't a mistress another form of lackey?'

'Mistress! Good lord, what a delightfully old-fashioned word. But I like it. Mistress,' he repeated thoughtfully. 'Yes, you would make me a perfect mistress. *Now*.' And with a wicked gleam in his eye, he put her fingers to his lips once more.

Tara pulled her hand away. She might have hit him if the lift doors hadn't opened at that moment.

A brunette was standing there, waiting for the lift. A strikingly attractive brunette with big brown eyes, eyes which grew bigger when they saw Max, then narrowed as they shifted over to Tara.

Max's fingers tightened around Tara's.

'Hello, Max,' the brunette said first. 'Long time, no see.'

'Indeed,' Max replied, but said no more.

Tara could feel the tension gripping all of Max's body through his hand. No, not tension. Hostility. He hated this woman, for whatever reason. Why? Had he loved her once?

Tara stared at the brunette more closely, trying to guess her age for one thing. Impossible to tell accurately. Maybe mid-to late-twenties. She had the sleek look of the very rich, which meant she might be older. Weekly visits to beauty salons could hold back the hands of time. Her face was clear of wrinkles and superbly made up. But her shoulder-length, shiny dark-brown hair was her crowning glory, framing her face in a layered bob with not a single strand out of place.

She made Tara conscious of her own hair, which

was scraped back from her face and pulled up high on her head into a tight knot, the only style she could manage in the small amount of time Max had given her to get ready. Less than fifteen minutes earlier, her whole head had been sopping wet.

'You're looking well,' the brunette addressed to Max.

'If you'll excuse us, Alicia,' Max said. 'We are already late for our dinner reservation.' And he ushered Tara away, stunning Tara with his rudeness. Ever since she'd met Max, she'd never known him to act like that with anyone.

Tara did not glance back, or say a word during the short walk from the lift to the restaurant. She remained discretely silent whilst the *maître d'* greeted them, then instructed their personal waiter—a good-looking young guy named Jarod—to show them to their table.

It was a very special table, reserved for special occasions and people who wanted total privacy from the other diners. Set in a back corner of the restaurant, the candlelit table was housed in a tiny room, which was dimly lit and very atmospheric.

The first time Max had brought her here, she'd thought it was so romantic. Subsequent visits had been just as romantic. Tonight, however, the encounter with the brunette had turned Tara's mind away from romance. Unless one could consider jealousy an element of romance. Max could say what he liked but the way that woman had looked at him—just for a moment—had been with the eyes of a woman who'd been more than a passing acquaintance, or an employee.

As the minutes dragged on—Max was spending an inordinate amount of time studying the drinks menu—her agitation increased. By the time the waiter departed and the opportunity presented itself to ask him about the infernal woman, Tara feared she was going to put her questions all wrong. She dithered over what to actually say.

'There's no need to be jealous,' Max pronounced abruptly. 'Alicia was Stevie's girlfriend, not mine.'

'I wasn't jealous,' Tara lied with a lift of her chin. 'Just bewildered by your rudeness. So what did this Alicia do to Stevie to make you hate her so much?'

'The moment my brother was diagnosed with testicular cancer, Alicia dumped him like a shot. Said she couldn't cope.'

Tara was stunned to see Max's hands tremble as he raked them through his hair.

'My God, *she* couldn't cope,' he growled. 'How did she think Stevie was going to cope when the girl he loved—and who he *thought* loved him—didn't stand by him through his illness? I blame her entirely for his treatment being unsuccessful. When she left him, he lost the will to live.'

'But I thought...'

'Yes, yes, I blame my father, too. But Alicia even more so. At least Dad never pretended a devotion to Stevie. When he didn't come home to be by his dying son's bedside, it wasn't such a shock. Not to Stevie, anyway. He told me just days before he died that Dad didn't love him the way he loved me.' Max's deeply set blue eyes looked haunted. 'God, Tara, do you know how I felt when he said that? Stevie, who was such a good boy, who'd never hurt anyone in his life. How could any father not love him more than me? I wasn't a patch on my little brother.'

Tara frowned. Max had told her ages ago about the circumstances surrounding his younger brother's tragic death. Yet he'd never mentioned Stevie's girl-friend's part in it.

'Why didn't you tell me about Alicia, Max? You told me what your father did.'

'I don't like to talk about Stevie. I told you as much as I had to, to explain why I didn't invite you home to visit my parents, especially last Christmas. Alicia was irrelevant to that explanation,' he finished brusquely. 'Aah, here's the champagne.'

Tara wasn't totally satisfied with Max's explanation but stayed silent whilst the waiter opened the bottle, poured them both a glass then finally departed after Max told him to return in ten minutes for their meal order.

'It's not like you to order champagne,' she said as she took a sip. Max usually ordered red wine.

'I thought we would share a bottle. To celebrate the anniversary of our meeting. It was a year ago today that I walked into Whitmore's. Of course, it was a Friday not a Saturday, but the date's spot-on.'

'Oh, Max, how sweet of you to remember!'

'I'm a sweet guy.'

Tara smiled. 'You can be. Obviously. But I wouldn't say sweetness is one of your best-known attributes.'

'No?' He smiled across the table, reminding her for the second time that night how very handsome he was. 'So what *is* my best-known attribute?'

She couldn't help it. She blushed.

Max laughed. 'I will take that as a compliment. Although you've hardly been able to compare, since I'm your one and only lover. At least, I presume I am. Though maybe not for long, after today.'

'What on earth do you mean by that?'

'Maybe you'll want to fly to other places. Experience other men.'

Tara stared at him. 'You don't know me very well if you think that. What happened earlier, Max, is because I love you deeply and trust you totally. I could never be like that with some other man. I would just die of embarrassment and shame.'

His eyes softened on her. 'You really mean that, don't you?'

'Of course I do!'

He shook his head. 'You're one in a million, Tara. There truly aren't many women like you out there for men like me. True love is a luxury not often enjoyed by the rich and famous. Our attractiveness lies in our bank balances, not our selves.'

'I don't believe that. You're far too cynical, Max.'

'I've met far too many Alicias not to be cynical. Do you know that within six months of telling Stevie she loved him but couldn't cope, she'd married another heir to a fortune? Then, when she'd divorced that sucker twelve months later, she even had the temerity to make a line for me one night when our paths crossed.'

'And?'

'And what?'

'Don't take me for a total fool, Max. Something happened between you two. I felt it.'

He sighed. 'You feel too much sometimes. OK, so I was in a vengeful mood that night. When Alicia started coming on to me, I played along with it. When I suggested leaving the party we were attending she jumped at the chance, even though she'd come with someone else. I took her to a club, where we drank and danced.'

Danced! Tara's stomach crunched down hard at the mere thought of another woman in her Max's arms. She knew it was before they'd met, but still...

'I waited for her to make her excuses about Stevie,' Max continued as he twisted his champagne glass round and round. 'I knew she would. But what she said really floored me. She told me that she'd only dated Stevie to be near me. She told me that she'd never really loved my brother. It was me she'd loved all along. She claimed she only married that other man because she thought she had no chance with me.

I told her what I thought of her and her so-called love
and walked out.'

Tara never said a word, because she suspected that
what the woman had said might be true. She'd seen
a photograph of Stevie and whilst he had been a nice-
looking boy, his face had lacked Max's strength and
charisma.

'Love is just a weapon to such women,' Max added
testily. 'My own mother pretends she still loves my
father, despite his having been a neglectful husband,
as well as a neglectful father. Why? Because it would
probably cost too much money to divorce him. I overheard her tell a lady friend once that she knew about
Dad's womanising ways, but turned a blind eye. Even
now that he's in a wheelchair, a wretched wreck of a
man, she stays with him, catering to his every need.
They're as bad as each other, bound together by their
greed and their lack of moral fibre. That's why I have
as little as possible to do with them these days. Both
of them make me sick.'

Tara was stunned by his outburst, and the depth of
his bitterness. Bitterness was never good for anyone's soul. Neither was revenge. It was very self-
destructive.

'But you could be wrong, Max,' she ventured quietly. 'Your mother might very well love your father.
There might be things you don't know. We rarely
know what goes on inside a marriage. I found that
out last weekend. I always thought my sister was unhappy in her marriage. She fell pregnant, you see,

during her last year at school. Dale wasn't much older, and still doing his plumbing apprenticeship. They got married, with Jen thinking she could finish her schooling. But she was too sick during her pregnancy to study. Then, when her first baby was barely six months old, she fell pregnant again. She's always complaining about her life, and her husband. She says he spends too much time and money drinking with his mates. But when I asked her why she didn't leave him and get a divorce, she looked at me as though I was mad. Told me she was *very* happy with Dale and would never dream of getting a divorce. So maybe you're wrong, Max. It *is* possible, you know,' she added with a wry little smile.

He smiled back. 'Possible. But not probable. Look, let's not spoil tonight with such talk. Let's just eat some wonderful food together and drink this wonderful champagne. I want to get you delightfully tipsy so that I can take you back upstairs and have my truly wicked way with you.'

Although Tara's stomach flipped at the prospect, she stayed calm on the surface, suspecting that Max was watching her for her reaction. As much as she was curious, she wasn't sure if the reality would be as exciting as the fantasy. And even if it was, what about the consequences? Did she really want Max thinking she would do *anything* he asked? What next?

'You think that's the answer to my co-operation?' she asked coolly. 'Getting me drunk?'

'Is it?'

'I hope not.'

'Then how about this?' And he extracted a small gold velvet box from his pocket.

Tara stared at the ring-sized box.

An engagement ring. He'd bought her an engagement ring. He was going to ask her to marry him!

The shot of adrenalin which instantly charged through her bloodstream made a mockery of her denial to her mother that marriage to Max was not what she wanted at this moment in her life.

Clearly, her body knew things which her brain did not.

'Go on,' he said, and reached over to put the gold box on the white tablecloth in front of her. 'Open it.'

Something about the scenario suddenly didn't fit Tara's image of how a man like Max would ask her to marry him. It was all far too casual. *He* was far too casual.

She sucked in a deep breath, then let it out slowly, gathering herself before opening the box. When she did, and her eyes fell upon a huge topaz dress ring, she was ready to react as she was sure Max expected her to react, with seeming pleasure and gratitude.

'Oh, Max, it's lovely! Thank you so much.'

'I knew it would match that dress. That's why I wanted you to wear it tonight. Go on,' he said eagerly. 'Put it on. See if it fits.'

She slipped it on the middle finger of her right hand.

'Perfect,' she said, and held it out to show him.

The diamond-cut stone sparkled under the candle-light. 'But you really shouldn't have, Max. You make me feel guilty that I didn't buy you anything. I had no idea you were such a romantic.'

'I think I'm catching the disease from you.'

'I don't know why you keep calling me a roman-tic.'

'When a girl of your looks reaches twenty-four still a virgin then I know she's a romantic.'

'Maybe. Maybe not. I consider myself more of an idealist. I didn't want to have sex till I *really* wanted it. I wasn't waiting for love to strike so much as pas-sion. Which it did. With you. I didn't realise I was in love with you till the following morning. How long did it take till you realised you loved me?'

'The moment you smiled at me in that shop I was a goner.'

'Oh, Max, now who's being the romantic?'

He smiled. 'Aah, here comes Jarod to take our or-der. Let me order for you tonight, darling. Now that you're breaking out in other ways, I think it's time you tried some different foods.'

'If you insist.'

He grinned. 'I insist.'

Tara sat back and sipped her champagne whilst Max went to town with their meal order. He'd always liked ordering the rarest and most exotic foods on the menu for himself.

Clearly, Max was happier now with her than ever. Tara glanced down at the topaz ring and told herself it had been silly of her to want it to be an engagement ring.

Max was right. She *was* a romantic.

'You don't like it,' Max said.

Tara glanced up to see that Jarod had departed and Max was looking at her with a worried frown.

'Of course I do,' she said with a quick smile. 'It's gorgeous.'

'So what were you thinking about that made you look so wistful?'

She shrugged. 'I guess I'd like to spend more time with the wonderful man who gave it to me.'

'Your wish is my command, my darling. How would you like to quit that job of yours and come with me when I go overseas?'

Tara's mouth dropped open.

'I take it that stunned look on your face means a yes?'

'I... I... Yes. Yes, of course. But Max, are you sure?'

'I wouldn't have asked you if I wasn't sure.'

So why haven't you asked me this before now?

The question zoomed into her mind like an annoying bee, buzzing around in her brain, searching for the truth. What had changed in their relationship that he suddenly wanted her with him all the time?

Tara hated the answer that would not be denied.

The sex. The sex between them had changed.

'Why now, Max?' she couldn't stop herself asking whilst her stomach had tightened into a knot.

He shrugged. 'Do you want the truth? Or romantic bulldust?'

'Romantic bulldust, of course.'

He laughed. 'OK. I love you. I love you so much that I can no longer stand leaving you behind when I go away. I want you with me, every day. I want you in my bed, every night. How's that?'

'Pretty good. Now how about the truth?'

Max looked at her and knew he would never tell her the truth, which was that he was afraid of losing her if he left her behind. He suspected she had never felt anything like she'd felt with him today. How, now, could he expect her to patiently wait for him to come home? She might not actively look for other lovers, but men would always pursue Tara…

'The truth,' he repeated, doing his best to look in command of the situation. 'The truth is I love you, Tara. I love you so much I can't stand the thought of leaving you behind when I go away. I want you with me, every day. I want you in my bed, every night.'

And wasn't *that* the truth!

Tara tried not to burst into tears. She had a feeling that sobbing all over the place was not what Max wanted in a mistress. Because of course, if she did this, if she quit her job and let Max pay for everything whilst she travelled with him, that was what she would be. Possibly, that was all she would ever be. There was no guarantee their relationship would end in marriage, no matter how much Max said he loved her.

Still, there'd never been any guarantees of that. He'd never given her any. And he wasn't giving her any now.

Tara thought of what her mother had said about how he would *never* give her what she wanted. Once again, she tried to pin down in her mind what she actually wanted from Max at this stage in her life. That ring business had rocked her a bit. Suddenly, she wasn't at all sure. The only thing she *was* sure of was that she didn't want to lose Max. Now more than ever.

'I'll have to give Whitmore's two weeks' notice,' she said, her voice on the suddenly breathless side. Her heart was racing madly and her mouth had gone dry. 'I can't just leave them in the lurch. February is top tourist season for the Japanese.'

'Fine. But what about next weekend? I have to go back to Auckland, negotiate with some owners there about a hotel. If I arrange plane tickets for you, would you join me there?'

'I wouldn't be able to leave till the Saturday morning. We'd only have the one night together.'

'Better than nothing,' he said, blue eyes gleaming in the candlelight.

'Yes,' she agreed, a tremor ripping down her spine. By next Saturday, her body would be screaming for him.

She picked up her glass and took a decent swallow, aware that he was watching her closely.

'Are you all right, Tara?' he asked, softly but knowingly, she thought.

'No,' she returned sharply. 'No, I'm not. And it's all your fault. I feel like a cat on a hot tin roof.'

'Aaah.'

There was a wealth of satisfaction—and knowledge—in that aaah.

'Would you like me to have our meals sent up to the penthouse?'

Tara blinked, then stared at him. If she blindly said yes, it would be the end of her. She would be his in whatever way he wanted her. There would be no further questioning over what *she* wanted, because what she wanted would be what *he* wanted.

But how could she say no when she wanted it too? To be his. To let him take her back into that world he had shown her today, that dizzying, dazzling world where sensation was heaped upon sensation, where giving pleasure was as satisfying as receiving it, where the mind was set free of worry and all its focus was centred on the physical.

'Can we take the champagne too?' she heard herself saying, shocked to the core at how cool her voice sounded.

'Absolutely.' Max was already on his feet.

'Will you still respect me in the morning?' she said with a degree of self-mockery as he walked round the table towards her.

Placing one hand under her chin, he tipped up her face for a kiss which was cruel in its restraint.

He's teasing me, she realised. Giving me a taste of what's to come.

'Tell me you love me,' he murmured when his mouth lifted.

'I love you.'

'Let's go.'

CHAPTER SEVEN

'I'M BEING punished for last night,' Tara groaned.

'You've just got a hangover,' Max reassured her, sitting down on the side of the bed and stroking her hair back from her forehead. 'You must have had too much champagne.'

'I'll never touch the stuff again,' Tara said, not sure which was worse. Her headache or her swirling stomach.

'Pity,' Max said with a wry smile. 'You really were *very* cooperative.'

'Don't remind me.'

Max laughed. 'I'll get you a couple of painkillers and a glass of water.'

Max disappeared into the bathroom, leaving Tara with her misery and her memories of the night before. Impossible to forget what she had allowed. Ridiculous to pretend that she hadn't thrilled to it all.

Tara groaned, then groaned again. She was going to be sick.

Her dash to the bathroom was desperate, shoving Max out of the way. She just had time to hold her hair back and out of the way before everything came up that she'd eaten the night before. It came up and came up till she was left exhausted and shaken.

It's just a hangover, she told herself as Max helped her over to the basin, where she rinsed out her mouth and washed her face. Or the same virus I had yesterday morning. I couldn't possibly be pregnant. Mum put that silly thought into my head. And it *is* silly. I had a period, for pity's sake.

'Poor darling,' Max comforted as he carried her back to bed and placed her still naked body gently inside the sheets. When she started shivering he covered her up with a quilt and tucked it around her. 'No point taking any tablets if you're throwing up. I'll go get you that glass of water. And a cool washer to put on your forehead. That helps sometimes. Take it from one who knows. I've had a few dreadful hangovers in my time. Still, you must be extra-susceptible to champagne, because you didn't have *that* much. I think I had the major share. And we wasted a bit. On you.'

'Don't remind me about that, either,' she said wretchedly. 'Could you dispose of that disgusting champagne bottle? I don't want to look at it.'

'Come, now, Tara, you loved it last night. *All* of it,' he said as he swept the empty bottle off the bedside table and headed for the doorway. 'But I will tolerate your morning-after sensitivities,' he tossed over his shoulder, 'in view of your fragile condition.'

Her fragile condition...

Tara bit her bottom lip as the question over her being sick for a second morning in a row returned to haunt her. Max was right. She hadn't had that much champagne. Hard to pin her hopes on the gastric virus going around, either. With that, Jen and her kids had been running to use the loo all the time. Then there was her sudden recovery yesterday afternoon and evening, only for her to become nauseous again this morning.

If she hadn't had a period recently then she would have presumed she was pregnant, as her mother had. Was it possible to have a period and still be pregnant? Tara had read of a few such cases. They weren't proper periods, just breakthrough bleeding, mostly related to women who'd fallen pregnant whilst on the Pill. Nothing was a hundred per cent safe, except abstinence. Her mother had told her *that,* too.

'Oh, God,' she sobbed, and stuffed a hand into her mouth.

'That bad, huh?' Max said as he strode back into the bedroom, carrying a glass of water with some ice in it. 'Do you want me to ring the house medico? I have one on call here at the weekends.'

'No! No doctor.'

'OK, OK,' Max soothed, coming round to place the glass on the bedside table. 'No doctor. I'm just trying to help. I don't like seeing you this sick.'

'What you don't like is not having your new little sex slave on tap this morning!'

The horrible words were out of her mouth before she could stop them. She saw Max's head jerk back. Saw the shock in his eyes.

Tara was truly appalled at herself. 'I'm sorry,' she

cried. 'I didn't mean that. Truly. I'm not myself this morning. I'm a terrible person when I'm sick.' And when I'm petrified I might be pregnant.

The very thought sent her head whirling some more. She didn't want to be pregnant. Not now. Not when Max had just asked her to travel with him. Not when her life had just become so exciting.

'It's all right, Tara. I understand.'

'No, no, you don't.'

'I think I do. What happened yesterday. And last night. It was a case of too much too soon. I became greedy. I should have taken things more slowly with you. You might have enjoyed yourself at the time, but hindsight has a way of bringing doubts and worries. It's good, in a way, that this morning has given us both a breather. Even if it's not under pleasant circumstances for you.'

'You don't mind?'

His smile was wry. 'Mind? Of course I mind. I'd love to be making love to you right at this moment. But I'm a patient man. I can wait till next weekend. And next time, I promise I won't frighten you with my demands.'

'You...you didn't frighten me, Max.'

He stared into her eyes. 'No? Are you sure?'

'I'm sure. I liked everything we did together.'

He let out a sigh of relief. 'I'm so glad to hear that. I have to confess I was a bit worried that I might have gone too far last night. Not at the time. But when I woke, this morning.'

Not as worried as *she* was this morning.

Max sat down beside her on the bed and started stroking her head again. 'Still, I don't want you to ever think you have to do anything you don't want to do, Tara. I love *you,* not just having sex with you. All right?'

She nodded, but tears threatened. Max might say that now, but what if she *was* pregnant? Would he be so noble when faced with her having his baby? Or would he do and say things which might threaten their relationship for good?

Endless complications flooded into her mind, almost overwhelming her with fear, and feelings of impending doom.

But you don't *know* you're pregnant, she tried telling herself. You could very well be wrong.

Yes, yes, she would cling to that thought. At least till Max left. She couldn't continue thinking and acting this way or she would surely break down and blurt out what was bothering her. And she really didn't want to do that. Max had enough things on his mind these days without burdening him with premature news of an unconfirmed pregnancy.

No, she had to pull herself together and stop being such a panic artist. Max had a couple of hours yet before he left for the airport. Surely she could stay calm for that length of time. Why spoil the rest of his stay with negativity and pessimism? What would that achieve? He was being so sweet and understanding this morning. It wasn't fair to take her secret fears out on him, especially when it was only a guess, and based on nothing but her feeling nauseous two mornings in a row.

Hardly conclusive proof.

'Max…'

'Yes?'

'I'm feeling a bit better now. My stomach is much more settled. Do you think I should try something to eat? Maybe some toast?'

'I think that would be an excellent idea. Eating is another good cure for a hangover. I'll have Room Service send some up.' And he stood up to walk round to the extension that sat on his bedside chest. 'I'll order myself a decent breakfast at the same time. Just coffee won't cut it this morning. Not with airline food beckoning me later today. I need something far more substantial.'

Tara pulled herself up into a sitting position, dragging the sheet up with her over her breasts and tucking it modestly around her. As much as she might have discovered a new abandon when she was turned on, she was still not an exhibitionist.

'You know, Max,' she said when he'd finished ordering, 'you should keep some staple foods in your kitchen. Cereals last for weeks. So does long-life milk and juice. And bread freezes. It's rather extravagant to order everything you eat from Room Service.'

'Maybe, but I intend to keep on doing it. I work incredibly long hours and I have no intention of spending my precious leisure time in the kitchen. I have far more enjoyable things to do when I'm on R & R.' And he gave her a wickedly knowing smile.

Tara was taken aback. Maybe she was extra-sensitive this morning, but she didn't like Max describing the time he spent with her as R & R—rest and recreation.

She dropped her eyes to her lap to stop his noting her negative reaction and found herself staring at the huge topaz ring which was still on her finger. His gift was the only thing he hadn't removed from her last night.

Suddenly, she saw it not as an anniversary present, but the beginning of many such gifts, given to her for services rendered; rewards for travelling with him and filling his rest and recreation hours in the way he liked most.

She pictured their sex games being played out in lavish hotel rooms all over the world, Max's demands becoming more and more outrageous in line with the extravagance of his gifts. Soon, she'd be dripping in diamonds and designer clothes. But underneath, she wouldn't be wearing *any* underwear. In the end, she would become his sex slave for real, bought and paid for, fashioned to fulfil his every desire. She would cease to be her own person. She'd just be a possession. A toy, to be taken out and played with during Max's leisure time, and ignored when he went back to his real life. His work.

Of course, such a sex toy had to be perfect, physically. It could never be allowed to get fat. Or pregnant.

Pregnant sex slaves had two choices. They either got rid of their babies. Or they themselves were dispensed with.

Both scenarios horrified Tara.

'Max!' she exclaimed, her eyes flying upwards.

But Max was no longer in the bedroom. Tara had been so consumed with her thoughts—and her imaginary future—that she hadn't noticed his leaving.

'Max!' she called out and the door of his dressing room opened. He emerged, dressed in one of his conservative grey business suits, though not teamed with his usual white shirt today. His shirt was a blue, the same blue as his eyes. And his tie was a sleek, shiny silver, a change from his usual choice. His hair was still damp from a recent shower and slicked straight back from his head.

He looked dashing, she thought. And very sexy.

But then, Max *was* very sexy.

An image flashed into her mind of his tipping champagne from the bottle over her breasts, then bending to lick it off. Slowly. So very slowly. She'd pleaded with him to stop teasing her.

But he'd ignored her pleas.

That was part of the game, wasn't it?

The best part. The most exciting part.

'What?' he asked, frowning over at her.

'I… I didn't know where you were,' she said lamely, hating herself for her sudden weakness. She'd been going to tell him that she'd changed her mind about travelling with him; that she didn't really like the way things were heading.

But the words had died in her throat at the sight of him. It was so true what they said. The mind could be willing but the flesh was very weak.

'Thought I might as well get dressed before Room Service called,' he explained. 'I know how you don't like the butler coming in when you're in bed. Besides, no point in staying in my bathrobe with you feeling under the weather, is there?'

The front door bell rang right at that moment. Max hurried from the room, returning in no time, wheeling a traymobile. By then, Tara had decided she was being a drama queen. Max loved her and she loved him. It was only natural that he would ask her to travel with him. And it was only natural that she would go.

As for her pregnancy...

That was as far-fetched an idea as her becoming some kind of mindless sex slave. She had always had a strong sense of her own self. Her mother called her wilful and her sister said she was incredibly stubborn. If Max started crossing the line where she was concerned, she would simply tell him so and come home. Nothing could be simpler.

'Now, that's what I like to see,' Max said as he tossed her one of the Sunday papers. 'Almost a happy face.'

She smiled at him. 'Nothing like feeling better to make you feel better.'

He scowled. 'Now she tells me, *after* I'm dressed.'

'That was not an invitation for more sex, Max Richmond. I think we've indulged enough for one weekend. I would hate to think that all I'd be if and when I travel with you is a means of rest and relaxation.'

He frowned at her. 'If and when? Did I hear correctly? I thought you'd agreed to come with me. It was just a matter of giving your notice.'

'Yes, well, I've been having some second thoughts.'

Tara knew how to play that game. The hard-to-get game.

For years before she'd met Max, she'd played it to the hilt. Whilst she'd not been so successful with Max, she suspected that it would do him good to be a little less sure of her.

'Aah,' he said. 'I see. Hence, the sex-slave accusation.'

'Yes...'

Max sighed, then came over to sit on the bed once more.

'I don't know how many times I have to tell you this weekend, Tara, but I love you. Deeply. I want you with me for more than just sex. I enjoy just being with you, even when we're not making love. I enjoy your company and your conversation. I enjoy your wit and your charm with other people. Taking you out is a delight. *You* are a delight. When you're not sick, that is,' he added drily, dampening her pleasure in his compliments.

'Charming,' she said. 'So if I ever get sick, I will be tossed aside, like a toy whose batteries have run low?'

'No more of this nonsense!' he pronounced, and rose to his feet. 'You're coming with me and that's that. So what would you like on your toast? There is a choice of honey, Vegemite and jam. Strawberry jam, by the look of it.'

'Vegemite.'

'Vegemite toast coming up, then.'

Tara raised no further objections to travelling with him.

But she resolved not to ever let him take away her much valued sense of independence. She'd always been her own person and would hate to think that her love for Max would eventually turn her into some kind of puppet.

She munched away on her toast and watched him tuck into his huge breakfast, which he ate whilst sitting with her on the bed. He chatted away when he could, pleasing her with the news that the comment she'd made yesterday about never being able to resist a buy-one, get-one-free sale had inspired him to make such an offer with his hotel in Hong Kong.

Stay one week, get one free was now posted on its website and was already bringing in results with scads of bookings.

'We won't make a great profit on the accommodation,' he told her. 'But empty rooms don't return a cent. Hopefully, the type of guest this promotion attracts will spend all the money they think they've saved in other places in the hotel. Pierce thought I was crazy, but that was yesterday. This morning he's singing my praises. Says I'm a genius. Forgive me for not telling him that my little genius is my girlfriend. Male ego is a terrible thing.'

Tara suspected that it was.

But it was also an attractive thing. It gave Max his competitiveness, and his drive. It made him the man he was, the man she loved.

'Isn't it unusual to have a male PA?' she remarked, somewhat idly.

'Unusual maybe. But wise, given the amount of time we spend overseas together.'

Tara blinked as the meaning behind Max's words sank in. 'Did you hire Pierce *because* he's a man?'

'You mean because I didn't want to risk becoming involved with a female secretary?'

'Yes.'

'Absolutely. Been there, done that, and it was messy.'

'How long ago?'

'A good year or so before I met you.'

'Did you sleep with her?'

Max pulled a face. 'I wish you hadn't asked me that.'

'Did you sleep with her?'

'Once or twice.'

'Was it once, or twice?'

'More than that, actually. Look, it was messy, as I said.'

'Tell me about it.'

He sighed. 'I'd rather not.'

'I want to know. You know all about my past.'

'Tara, you don't *have* a past.'

'Yes, I do. I might not have slept with guys but I made out with quite a few. I told you all about them that first night. I want to know, Max. Tell me.'

'OK, but it isn't pretty.'

'Was *she* pretty?'

'Pretty? No, Grace was not pretty. Not plain, either. Very slim. Nicely groomed. With red hair. Out of a bottle. She was already my personal assistant when Dad had his stroke. Up till then I'd taken care of the money side of things in the firm, here at home in Sydney. Suddenly, I had to go overseas. A lot. I took her with me. The man she was living with at the time didn't like it and broke up with her. We'd never been involved before but all of a sudden, we were together every day of the week. We were both lonely, and stressed out. One night, over too many drinks, she made a pass at me and it just happened. It wasn't love on my part. And she said it wasn't on hers. It was more a matter of mutual convenience. I should have stopped it. I still feel guilty that I didn't. Finally, when I tried to, she told me she was pregnant.'

Tara sucked in sharply.

'She wasn't,' he went on. 'It was just a ploy to get

me to marry her. Frankly, I was suspicious right from the start. I'd always used condoms and there'd never been an accident, not like that one I had with you last year. When I insisted on accompanying her to a doctor to find out how far pregnant she was, she broke down and confessed she wasn't at all.'

'And if she had been, Max? What then? What would you have done?'

He shrugged. 'I honestly don't know. But she wasn't, so I didn't have to face that dilemma. Thank God. But it made me wary, I can tell you. Hence, Pierce.'

'I see. And what happened to her?'

'I'm pleased to say she went back home to the man she'd been living with before. I had a note from her some months later to say they were getting married, and this time she really was having a baby. I was happy for her because I suspect she thought she was past having a child. She wasn't all that young, you see. She was forty by then.'

'An older woman,' Tara said with an edge to her voice. 'And an experienced one, I'll bet. Did you learn some of those kinky games from her, Max? Was that why you couldn't stop? Because she never had to be persuaded to finish anything she started?'

'Stop it, Tara,' Max snapped. 'Stop it right now. You have no reason to be jealous of Grace. I'm sorry my past is not as pure as yours but I won't be cross-questioned on it. And I won't apologise for it. I'm a mortal man. I've made mistakes in my life, but hopefully I have learned from them.'

Putting aside his breakfast tray, he stood up. 'I think perhaps I should get going before you find something else to argue about. I can see you're out of sorts this morning in more ways than one. When you do feel well enough to go home, for pity's sake use the credit card I gave you to take a taxi this time. I noticed in the statements I receive that you never use the darned thing these days.'

'Fine,' she said, wanting him to just go so that she could cry.

His eyes narrowed on her. 'I wish I knew what was going on in that pretty head of yours.'

'Not much. Blonde-bimbo mistresses aren't known for their brains.'

'Tara…'

'I know. I'm acting like a fool. Forgive me.' Tears pricked at her eyes.

'Oh, Tara…' And he started walking towards her.

She knew, without his saying a word, that he was going to take her into his arms. If he did that, she was going to disintegrate and say even more stupid things.

'Please don't come near me,' she said sharply. 'I smell of sick.'

He stopped, his eyes tormented. 'I don't want to leave you on this note.'

'You can make it up to me next weekend in Auckland, when I feel better.'

'That's a week away.'

'Ring me from Hong Kong, then. But not tonight. Tonight I want to go to bed early and sleep. I'm wrecked.'

He smiled. 'Same here. I'll be sleeping on that plane. All right, I'll ring you tomorrow night. Can I peck you on the forehead?'

'If you must.'

'Oh, I must,' he said softly as his lips brushed over her forehead. 'I must...'

Tara waited till he was definitely gone before she dissolved into some very noisy weeping.

CHAPTER EIGHT

TARA stared at the blue line, all her fears crystallised.

She was pregnant.

Stumbling back from the vanity basin, she sank down onto the toilet seat, her head dropping into her hands.

But somehow, she was beyond tears. She'd cried for ages after Max left. Cried and cried.

It had been close to two o'clock by the time she'd pulled herself together enough to get dressed and go downstairs to buy a pregnancy-testing kit from the chemist shop in the foyer.

And now there was no longer any doubt. Or guessing. She was going to have Max's baby.

Tara shook her head from side to side. It wasn't fair. She'd taken every precaution. This shouldn't be happening to her. What on earth was she going to do?

Tara sucked in deeply as she lifted her head. What *could* she do?

Nothing. The same way Jen had done nothing when Dale had got her pregnant. The Bond sisters hadn't been brought up to have abortions.

Not that Tara wanted to get rid of Max's baby. If she could just get past her fear over what Max would say and do when he found out, she might even feel happy about it.

But that was her biggest problem, wasn't it?

Telling Max.

What if he accused her of deliberately getting pregnant? Even worse, what if he demanded she get a termination?

That would be the death knell of their relationship, she knew. Because it would prove to her once and for all that he didn't really love her.

A huge wave of depression washed through her, taking Tara lower than she'd ever been in her life before. If she discovered Max didn't really love her, how could she stand it? How would she cope?

You'll have to cope, girl, came back the stern answer. You're going to become a mother. You're going to be needed. Having some kind of breakdown is simply not on.

Tara squared her shoulders as her self-lecture had some effect. But when she thought of having to tell her own mother about the baby she wilted again.

Not yet, Tara decided with a shudder. She couldn't tell her yet. Maybe she wouldn't tell Max yet, either. First babies didn't show for quite a while. Maybe she could delay the confrontation with Max till she was over four months, past the safe time for a termination. As much as Tara was confident he couldn't succeed in talking her into an abortion, she didn't want him to even try.

Unfortunately, she had no idea just how far pregnant she actually was. That was her first job. To find out.

Jen, Tara thought with a lifting of spirit. Jen had a nice doctor that she'd gone to when she was having her babies. Tara had gone with her a couple of times and had really liked him. On top of that, Jen wouldn't be too shocked, or read her the Riot Act. How could she when she'd got pregnant herself when she'd only been seventeen?

Yes, she would tell Jen, then ask her to arrange an appointment with her doctor. Preferably for this week, *before* her supposed trip to New Zealand. Tara need to know where things stood. Though really, unless her morning sickness went away, she couldn't see herself going anywhere overseas for ages.

Tara stood up and returned to the bedroom, where she sat down on Max's side of the bed and picked up the phone. After pressing the number for an outside line, she was about to punch in Jen's number when she realised she hadn't called her mother at all this weekend. Yet she'd promised to let her know when she'd be back.

Tara sighed. Really, once Max was on the scene, she couldn't think about anything or anyone else. The man had obsessed her these last twelve months. He probably would have obsessed her more after this incredible weekend, if his baby hadn't come along to put a halt to the proceedings. As much as she had thrilled to his forceful lovemaking—and it didn't seem to have hurt the baby—she really couldn't let him continue to make love to her in such a wild fashion.

Which meant her idea of keeping the baby secret for weeks wouldn't work. Max wouldn't understand why she wanted him to go back to his former style of slow, gentle lovemaking all of a sudden.

No. She would have to tell him the truth. And soon.

Now Tara wasn't sure whether to view this pregnancy as a saviour, or one huge sacrifice all round. No travelling overseas. No adventurous sex. Possibly, no Max at all!

Her chin trembled at this last thought.

Oh, life was cruel. Too cruel.

Tara slumped down on the bed and burst into tears again, the phone clutched in her hands. This time, her crying jag was considerably shorter than the last. Only ten minutes or so.

I'm definitely getting it together, she told herself as she dabbed at her eyes with the sheet, then took several gathering breaths.

'Time to ring Mum,' she said aloud, proud of her firm voice, and her firm finger. The number entered, she waited for her mother to answer.

'Hi there.'

'Oh. Oh, Jen. It's *you*!'

'Hi, Tara. Yep. It's me. I came over to visit Mum. She seemed a bit down. Dale's minding the kids. We're playing Scrabble and eating far too much cake. I presume his lord and master is in town?'

'Er— *Was.* He's gone now.'

'Brother, he doesn't stay long these days, does he?'

'Jen, can we talk? I mean…can Mum hear what you're saying?'

'Hold it a sec. Mum, it's Tara… Tara, Mum wants to know when you're coming home.'

'Shortly.'

'Shortly, Mum,' Tara heard Jen say. 'Why don't you go make us a cuppa while I have a chat with my little sister? I haven't talked to Tara in ages. Great. I'm alone now, Tara,' she said more quietly. 'What's up?'

'I… I'm pregnant.'

Jen stayed silent for a second, then just said, 'Bummer.'

'Is that it? Just *bummer*? I was hoping for some words of sympathy and wisdom.'

'Sorry. It was the shock. So how did this happen? I mean, I know how it *happened.* You had sex. I meant…did you forget the Pill one day or something?'

'Nope. Took it right on the dot every day.'

'Now, that is a real bummer. I was at least stupid and careless when I fell pregnant. Oh, Tara, what are you going to do?'

'Have my baby. The same way you did.'

'Yeah. We're suckers for doing the right thing, aren't we? So does Max know yet? I presume not.'

'No. I only found out myself a few minutes ago. The test went bluer than blue.'

'What do you think he'll say?'

'My head goes round and round every time I think about that. He's not going to be happy.'

'Men are never happy over unexpected pregnancies. But if he loves you, he'll stick by you. Dale went ballistic at first but after a while he calmed down, and really he was like a rock after that. Much better than me, actually. I cried for weeks and weeks.'

'I remember.'

'Do you think Max might ask you to marry him?'

'He's made it clear that marriage and kids are definitely not on his agenda, so your guess is as good as mine.'

'No, it isn't, Tara. You know the man. I don't. Does he love you?'

'He says he does.'

'You don't sound convinced.'

Tara sighed. 'I'm a bit mixed up about Max at the moment.'

'Is the pregnancy causing that, or what's going on in your relationship right now? Mum told me he's hardly ever around any more.'

Tara resented having to defend Max but, in fairness to the man, she felt she should. 'He's been very busy with all the world crises in the tourist industry. On the plus side, he did ask me just this weekend to quit my job and travel with him in future.' Tara didn't add that she was more qualified for the role of travelling companion since finding her sexual wings.

'Wow! And what did you say to that? Silly question. Yes, of course. I know you're crazy about the man.'

'I can't see myself travelling at all in the near future. I'm sick as a dog every morning. I need to see a doctor, Jen. Do you think you could get an appointment with your doctor this week?'

'He might be able to fit you in. But he won't be able to cure you of morning sickness. You'll just have to ride that out. Have a packet of dry biscuits by your bed and eat a couple before you get up. That helps. So, how far gone are you?'

'That's another thing. I don't know. Before this weekend, I hadn't seen Max in almost a month. Yet I had a period whilst he was away. At least, I thought I did. There was some bleeding when my period was due.'

'Yeah, that can happen. You're probably about six weeks gone if you're chucking up. But you need to have it checked out. Don't worry. I'll explain to the receptionist that it's an emergency. Now, when are you going to tell lover-boy?'

'Max,' Tara corrected firmly. 'Call him Max.'

'I'd like to call him lots of things, actually. But Max isn't one of them. Look, once you've been to the doctor and had things properly confirmed, you *have* to tell him. Even if he doesn't want to marry you, he's legally required to support this baby. You have no idea how much having children costs these days. Do you have private health cover?'

'For pity's sake, Jen, do you have to be so…so… pragmatic? I've just found out I'm having a baby. It's a very emotional time for me.'

'You can be emotional later. First things first, which is your welfare and the welfare of your child. Trust me. I know better than you in this.'

'I wish I hadn't told you at all!'

'Don't be ridiculous. You need all the support you can get. Which reminds me. You really should tell Mum.'

'Are you kidding? I'm going to delay that disaster area for as long as possible. Promise me you won't tell her, Jen. Right now. *Promise.*'

'OK. I think you're wrong, but it's your call. Speaking of calls, I'll ring the surgery first thing tomorrow morning. Then I'll ring you at work to let you know. I'll come with you, of course.'

'Would you? Oh, Jen, that would be great. I…I feel kind of… Oh, I don't know. I just can't seem to get my head around all this. A baby, for heaven's sake. I'm going to have a baby!' Tears threatened again.

'A beautiful baby, I'll warrant. And you'll love it to pieces.'

Tara gulped down the lump in her throat. 'Will I? I've never thought of myself as good mother material. I'm too…restless.'

'You just didn't know what you wanted. Having a baby will bring your life into focus. Er—we'd better sign off now before Mum comes back.'

'Yes, I really couldn't cope with the third degree

she'd give me. You won't forget to call me to-morrow?'

'I won't forget.'

'OK. Bye for now.'

Jen hung up, then grimaced up at her mother, who was standing there, mugs in hand.

'You heard that last bit, didn't you?'

Joyce nodded.

'She…she's too scared to tell you,' Jen said quietly, knowing by the look on her mother's face that she was about to have a hissy fit.

'But why?' Joyce wailed, putting the mugs down on the coffee-table next to the Scrabble board and flopping down into her chair.

'You know why, Mum. It's the same reason I didn't want to tell you when *I* was pregnant. Daughters want their mothers to be proud of them, not ashamed.'

'But Jen, I was never ashamed of you. Just disappointed for you. And worried. You were so young. And neither of you had any money.'

'What's age or money got to do with it? Love's what matters, Mum, when it comes to kids and marriage. Dale loved me and I loved him. We've had some tough times but we're going to make it. Unfortunately, I'm not so sure Max Richmond loves our Tara. Certainly not enough to give up his jet-setting lifestyle. That's why she's in such a tizz, because she knows it too. She's going to need a lot of support through this, Mum.'

'But how can I support her when I'm not supposed to even know?'

'She'll tell you. Just give her a little time.'

'From the sounds of things, she hasn't told Max Richmond.'

'Not yet. She's just found out herself, I gather, and he's not there.'

'He's never going to be there for her.'

'Probably. But he can be forced to support her financially. At least she won't be poor.'

'Yes, that's true. But Tara never wanted his money. You know she's not that kind of girl. She just wanted him to love her.'

'Yeah, I do know. She's always been a real romantic. She's been living in a fantasy world with her fantasy lover and now the real world has come up and bitten her, big time.'

Joyce was shaking her head. 'I've been afraid of something like this for a long time. If that man lets her down, I'm not sure she'll be able to cope.'

'She'll be upset, but she'll cope, Mum. You brought us up to be survivors. We're a stubborn pair. Trust me on that.'

'You're both good girls.'

'More's the pity. If Tara wasn't so damned good, she wouldn't have a problem.'

'Jen, you don't think she'd ever...'

'No. Never in a million years. She's going to have this baby whether lover-boy wants her to or not.'

Joyce looked shocked. 'You mean he might try to persuade her to get rid of it?'

'It's highly likely, don't you think?'

'She does love him a lot, Jen. If he puts the pressure on, she might do what he wants. Women in love can sometimes do things they regret later.'

'If he does that, *he'll* be the one to regret it,' Jen said fiercely. 'Tara would never forgive him, *or* herself. Look, I'd better drink this tea and get on home, Mum. Don't worry too much about Tara. Max can't put any pressure on her yet, because she doesn't intend telling him yet. OK?'

Joyce nodded, but inside she was beside herself with worry. Yet she could do nothing to help, because she wasn't supposed to know!

She glanced over at Jen and tried to work out why it was that daughters always misunderstood their mothers. All she wanted was for them to be happy.

Fancy Jen thinking she'd been ashamed of her when she fell pregnant. How could she possibly be ashamed of her daughters for doing exactly what she had done herself? Fallen madly in love. Maybe she would tell them one day that she had been pregnant when she'd married her beloved Bill.

Tears filled Joyce's eyes as she thought of the handsome man who'd swept her off her feet and into his bed before she could blink. How she'd loved that man. When he'd died, she could not bear to ever have another man touch her, though there'd been plenty who'd tried. Her daughters might be surprised to know that. But she'd only ever wanted her Bill.

'Please don't cry, Mum,' Jen said, reaching over to touch her mother's hand. 'Tara will be fine. You'll see.'

Joyce found a watery smile from somewhere. 'I hope so, love.'

'She's strong, is our Tara. And stubborn. Max won't find it easy to make her do anything she doesn't want to do. And she doesn't want to get rid of her baby. Come on, give me a hug and dry those tears. If you're all puffy-eyed when Tara gets home, she'll think I told you and then there'll be hell to pay. Promise me now that you won't let on.'

Joyce gave her daughter a hug and a promise. But it was difficult not to worry once she was alone, so she did the one thing she always did when she started to stress over one of her daughters. She took out the photo albums which contained the visual memories of all the good times they'd had as a family before her Bill died.

It always soothed her fears, looking at the man she'd loved so much and whom she still loved. She liked to talk to him; ask his advice.

He told her to hang in there, the way he always did. And to be patient. Some things took time. Time. And work. And faith.

She frowned over this last piece of advice. She had faith in Tara. The trouble was she had no faith in Max Richmond.

CHAPTER NINE

MAX replaced the receiver, a deep frown drawing his brows together. Something was wrong. He could feel it. He'd been feeling it all week.

Tara was different. Each night she'd cut his calls off after only a few minutes with some pitiful excuse. Her hair was wet. She wanted to watch some TV show. Tonight she'd said she had to go because she'd forgotten to feed her mother's cat and her mother was out playing bingo.

As if that couldn't have waited!

Then there was her definite lack of enthusiasm over their meeting up in Auckland. Tonight she'd even said she might not be able to make it. They were short-handed at Whitmore's this weekend and she felt obliged to help out. Would he mind terribly if she didn't come?

When he'd said that he definitely would, she'd sighed and said she would see what she could do, but not to count on her coming. She hadn't said she loved him before she ended the call, the way she usually did. Just a rather strained goodbye.

Last weekend had been a mistake, Max realised. He'd frightened her.

He shook his head. Hell, didn't she realise he didn't

really care about that kind of sex? All he wanted was to be with *her*.

He would ring her back, reassure her. It wasn't late. Only eight o'clock, her time.

When Mrs Bond answered the phone, he was startled. But not for long. Hadn't he subconsciously known Tara was lying to him?

'Max Richmond here, Mrs Bond. Can I speak to Tara, please?'

'No, you may not!' the woman snapped. 'I'm not going to let you upset her any more tonight. She's been through enough today.'

'What? But I didn't upset her tonight. And what do you mean she's been through enough today? What's going on that I don't know about?'

'Oh, Mum,' he heard Tara say in the background. 'How could you? You promised. I should never have told you.'

'He has to know, Tara. And the sooner the better. Why should you shoulder this burden all on your own?'

Max was taken aback. 'Burden? What burden? Speak to *me*, woman. Tell me what's going on.'

But she didn't answer him. All he heard was muffled sounds. His blood pressure soared as a most dreadful feeling of helplessness overwhelmed him. He wanted to be there, not here, hanging on the end of a phone thousands of miles away. If he was there, he'd make them both look at him and talk to him.

'Hey!' he shouted down the line. 'Is anyone there? Mrs Bond. Answer me, damn it!'

More sounds. A door slamming. A sigh.

'It's mé,' Tara said with another sigh.

'Thank heaven. Tara, tell me what's going on.'

'I suppose there's no point in keeping it a secret any longer. I'm pregnant, Max.'

'Pregnant!' He was floored. 'But how c—?'

'Before you go off on one,' she swept on rather impatiently, 'no, I didn't do this on purpose and no, I didn't even do it by accident. I took that darned Pill at the same time every day. I even had what I thought was a period a few weeks back. The doctor I saw today said that can happen. It's rare but not unheard-of. I'm about six or seven weeks gone, according to the ultrasound.'

A baby. Tara was going to have his baby. She wasn't tired of him, or frightened of him. She was just pregnant.

'Say something, for pity's sake!' she snapped.

'I was thinking.'

'I'll bet you were. Look, if you think I'm *happy* about this, then you're dead wrong. I'm not. The last thing I wanted at this time in my life was to have a baby. If being pregnant feels the way I've been feeling every morning then maybe I'll *never* want to have one.'

'So that's why you were sick the other morning!' Max exclaimed. 'It wasn't the champagne.'

'No, it wasn't the champagne,' she reiterated tetchily. 'It was *your* baby.'

'Yes, I understand, Tara. And your mother's right. This is my responsibility as much as it is yours. So how long have you known? You didn't know last weekend, did you?' Surely she wouldn't have encouraged him to act the way he had if she knew she was pregnant!

'No, of course I didn't. But when I woke up on the Sunday morning, chucking up two mornings in a row, I began to suspect.'

'Aah, so that's why you were so irritable with me that morning. I understand now. Poor baby.'

'Yes, it is a poor baby, to not be wanted by its parents.'

'You really *don't* want this baby?' His heart sank. When Grace had told him she was having a baby, he hadn't felt anything like what he was feeling now. He really wanted this child. It was his, and Tara's. A true love-child.

Tara's silence at the other end of the phone was more than telling. *He* might want their baby, but she didn't. She'd already raced off to a doctor to find out how far pregnant she was. Why? To see if it wasn't too late to have a termination?

Panic filled his heart.

'This is not the end of the world, Tara,' he said carefully. 'I don't want you making any hasty decisions. We should work this out together. Look, I won't go to New Zealand tomorrow. Pierce can handle that. I'll catch an overnight flight to Sydney. I should be able to get a seat. I'll catch a taxi straight out to your place as soon as I land and we'll sit down and work things out together. OK?'

Again, she didn't say a word.

'Tara…'

'What?'

The word was sharp. Sour, even. Max tried to understand how she felt, falling pregnant like that when she'd taken every precaution against it. She was only young, and just beginning to blossom, sexually speaking. She'd definitely been very excited about travelling with him. She probably felt her whole life was ruined with her being condemned to domestic boredom whilst he continued to jet-set around the world.

But having a termination was not the answer. Not for Tara. It would haunt her forever.

'Promise me you'll be there when I arrive,' he said. 'Even if the plane is late, promise me you won't go to work tomorrow.'

'Why should I make promises to you when you haven't made any to me? Go to hell, Max.' And she slammed the phone down in his ear.

Max gaped, then groaned once he saw what he'd done wrong. He should have told her again that he loved her. He should have reassured her straight away that he would be there for her, physically, emotionally and financially. Maybe he should have even asked her to marry her as a demonstration of his commitment to her and the child.

Of course, it wasn't an ideal situation, marrying because of a baby. He'd shunned marriage and children so far because he'd never wanted to neglect a family the way his father had. But the baby was a *fait accompli* and he truly loved Tara. Compromises could be made.

Yes, marriage was the answer. He would ring her back and ask her to marry him.

He swiftly pressed redial.

'Damn and blast!' he roared when the number was engaged.

Max tried her mobile but it was turned off. Clearly, she didn't want to speak to him. She was too angry. And she had every right to be. He was a complete idiot.

Max paced the hotel room for about thirty agitated seconds before returning to the phone and pressing redial once more. Again, nothing but the engaged tone. He immediately rang Pierce in the next room and asked him to get on to the airlines and find him a seat on an overnight flight to Sydney, money no object. He was to beg or bribe his way onto a plane.

'But what about New Zealand?' Pierce asked, obviously confused by these orders.

'You'll have to go there in my place,' Max said. 'Do you think you can handle that situation on your own?'

'Do I have complete authority? Or will I have to keep you in touch by phone during negotiations?'

'You have a free hand. You decide if the hotel is

a good buy, and if it is, buy it. At a bargain price, of course.'

'You kidding me?'

'No.'

'Wow. This is fantastic. To what do I owe this honour?'

'To my impending marriage.'

'Your what?'

'Tara's pregnant.'

'Good lord.'

Max could understand Pierce's surprise. Max was not the sort of man to make such mistakes. But he wasn't in the mood to explain the circumstances surrounding Tara's unexpected pregnancy.

'Just get on to the airlines, Pierce. Pronto. Then ring me back.'

'Will do. And boss?'

'Yes?'

'Thanks.'

'If you do a good job, there'll be a permanent promotion for you. And a lot more travelling. I'm planning on cutting down on my overseas trips in future. But first things first. Get me on a plane for Sydney. Tonight!'

Max didn't sleep much on the plane. Pierce had managed to get him a first-class seat on a QANTAS flight. He spent most of the time thinking, and planning. By the time the jumbo landed at Mascot soon after dawn, he had all his actions and arguments ready to convince Tara that marriage was the best and only option.

'A brief stop at the Regency Royale,' he told the taxi driver. 'Then I'm going on to Quakers Hill.'

The driver looked pleased. Quakers Hill was quite a considerable fare, being one of the outer western suburbs.

Max hadn't been out that way in ages, and what he saw amazed him. Where farms had once dotted the surrounding hillsides, there now sat rows and rows of new houses. Not small houses, either. Large, double-storeyed homes.

Tara's place, however, was not one of those. Her address was in the older section of Quakers Hill, near the railway station, a very modest fibro cottage with no garage and little garden to speak of. The small squares of lawn on either side of the front path were brown after the summer and what shrubs there were looked bedraggled and tired. In fact the whole house looked tired. It could surely do with a makeover. Or at least a lick of paint. But of course, Tara's mum was a widow, had been for a long time. She'd had no sons to physically help her maintain her home.

It suddenly struck Max as he opened the squeaky iron gate and walked up onto the small front porch that Tara's upbringing would not have been filled with luxuries. He recalled how awestruck she'd been the morning after the first night they'd spent together, when she'd walked through the penthouse and oohed and aahed at everything.

For the first time, a small doubt entered his mind about her falling pregnant. Could she be lying about it having been a rare accident? Could she have planned it? Was it a ploy to *get* him to marry her?

If it was, she would have to be the cleverest, most devious female he had ever known.

No, he decided as he rang the doorbell. The Tara he knew and loved was no gold-digger. She had a delightfully transparent character. She wasn't capable of that kind of manipulative behaviour. She was as different from the Alicias of this world as chalk was to cheese.

That was why he loved her so much.

The door opened and Max peered down into eyes which were nothing like Tara's. In fact, the short, plump, dark-haired woman glowering up at him was nothing like Tara at all, except perhaps for her nose. She had the same cute little upturned nose.

'You've wasted your time coming here, Mr Richmond,' she said sharply. 'You should have rung first.'

'I thought it best to speak to Tara in person. I did try to ring last night from the airport, but Tara must have taken the phone off the hook. She wasn't answering her mobile, either. Look, Mrs Bond, I can understand your feelings where I'm concerned. You think I'm one of those rich guys who prey on beautiful young girls, but you're wrong. I love your daughter and I would never do anything to hurt her. Now, could you tell her that I'm here, please?'

His words seemed to have taken some of the anger out of the woman's face. But she still looked concerned. 'That's what I'm trying to tell you. She's not here.'

'What? You mean she's gone to work, even after she knew I was coming?'

'No. She left here last night. Packed a bag and took a taxi to I don't know where.'

Max's astonishment was soon overtaken by frustration. The woman *had* to be lying. 'What do you mean you don't know where? That's crazy. You're her mother. She would have told you where she was going.'

A guilty colour zoomed into the woman's cheeks. 'We had an argument. She was angry with me for making her tell you about the baby. And I was angry with her for hanging up on you, then taking the phone off the hook. I thought she was being silly. And stubborn. I... I...'

Joyce bit her bottom lip to stop herself from crying. If only she could go back to yesterday. She'd handled the situation terribly from the moment Tara had told her about the baby. After the initial shock had worn off, she'd begun badgering the girl about telling Max and demanding that he marry her. When Tara threw back at her that men these days didn't marry girls just because they were pregnant, Joyce had been less than complimentary over the morals of men like Max Richmond, *and* the silly girls who became involved with them. By the time the man himself had rung last night, Joyce had been determined to somehow let him know that Tara was having his baby.

She'd thought she was doing the right thing. But she'd been wrong. It had not been her decision to make. Tara was a grown woman, even if Joyce had difficulty seeing her daughter as that. To her, she would always be *her* baby.

'I don't know where she's gone. Honestly, Mr Richmond,' she said, her head drooping as tears pricked at her eyes.

'Max,' he said gently, feeling genuinely sorry for the woman. 'I think it's about time you called me Max, don't you? Especially since I'm going to be your son-in-law.'

Joyce's moist eyes shot back up to his. 'You...you mean that? You're going to marry my Tara?'

'If she'll have me.'

'If she'll *have* you. The girl *adores* you.'

'Not enough to stay here when I asked her to.'

'I was partly to blame for that. I...I didn't handle the news of her pregnancy very well.'

'Don't worry, neither did I. Did she say something before she left?'

'She said to tell you she had to have some time by herself. Away from everyone telling her what to do. She said it was her body and her life and she needed some space to come to terms with the situation and work out what she was going to do. I spoke to Jen after she left. Jen's her older sister, by the way...'

'Yes, I know all about Jen.'

'You *do*?' Joyce was surprised.

Max's smile was wry. 'We do talk sometimes, Tara and I.'

The implication sent some pink into Joyce's cheeks. But truly, now that she'd met the man in the flesh, she couldn't blame Tara for losing her head over him. He was just so handsome. And impressive, with an aura of power and success about him. A wonderful dresser too. That black suit must have cost a small fortune.

'You were saying?' he prompted. 'Something about Tara's sister.'

'Oh, yes, well, I thought at first that Tara might have gone there, so I called Jen. I was probably on the phone when you rang from the airport. Tara had taken it off the hook but I put it back on later. Much later, I guess,' she added sheepishly. 'Anyway, she wasn't there and Jen didn't know where she might have gone. I was feeling awful because I thought I'd made her run away. But Jen said it was also because she was frightened you might try to talk her into getting rid of the baby when you got here.'

Max was appalled. But he could see that it wasn't an unreasonable assumption.

'And there I was,' he said wearily, 'worrying that *she* might do that.'

'Oh, no. Tara would never have an abortion. Never!'

'I'm glad to hear that. Because she'd never get over it, if she did. She's far too sweet and sensitive a soul.'

Joyce was touched that he knew Tara so well. This was not a man who wanted her daughter for her beauty alone. 'You…you really love Tara, don't you?'

'With all my heart. Clearly, however, she doesn't believe that. And I have only myself to blame. I've been thinking about our relationship all night on the plane and I can see I've been incredibly selfish and arrogant. People say actions speak louder than words, but not once did I stop to think what my actions were shouting to Tara. No wonder she had no faith in my committing to her and the baby. All I've ever given her were words. And words are so damned cheap. I have to show her now that I mean what I say. But first, I have to find her. Do you think you might invite me in for a cup of coffee, Mrs Bond, and we'll try to work out where she might have gone?'

'Joyce, Max,' she said with a smile which did remind him of Tara. 'If I'm going to be your mother-in-law, then I think you should call me Joyce.'

CHAPTER TEN

MAX waved Joyce goodbye through the taxi window, feeling pleased that he'd been able to make the woman believe that his intentions towards Tara were, at last, honourable. Not an easy task, given the way he'd treated her daughter this past year.

Joyce had not been backward in coming forward over his misdeeds. He was accused of having taken Tara for granted. Of neglecting her shamefully. But worst of all, of not caring enough to see how a girl like Tara would feel with his not making a definite commitment to her a lot sooner.

She'd poo-poohed Max's counter-arguments that Tara hadn't wanted marriage and children up till this point any more than he had.

'Tara needs security and commitment more than most girls,' she'd explained. 'She was more upset at losing her father than her older sister, yet Tara was only three at the time. She cried herself to sleep every night for months after the funeral. Having met you, I think, in a way, you are more than a lover to her. You are a father figure as well.'

Max hadn't been too pleased with this theory. It had made him feel old. He didn't entirely agree with it, either. Maybe Joyce didn't know her daughter as well as she thought she did. The grown-up Tara was a highly independent creature, not some cling-on. Yes, she was sensitive. And yes, she probably needed reassurance at this time in her life. But he didn't believe she thought of him as a father figure. Hell, she didn't even think of him as a father figure for their baby! If she had, she wouldn't have run away like this.

'Where in heaven's name *are* you, Tara?' he muttered under his breath.

'You say somethin', mate?' the taxi driver asked.

'Just having a grumble,' Max replied.

'Nothin' to grumble about, mate. The sun's out. We're winnin' the cricket. Life's good.'

Max thought about that simple philosophy and decided he could embrace it, if only he knew where Tara was.

He and Joyce decided she probably hadn't gone too far at night. Probably to a friend's house. The trouble was he'd discovered Tara had dropped all of her friends during the year she'd spent being his lady friend.

That was the term Joyce had tactfully used, although he had a feeling she was dying to use some other derogatory term, like mistress. Tara's mother hadn't missed an opportunity to put the knife in and twist it a little. Guilt gnawed away at him, alongside some growing frustration.

If Tara thought she could punish him this way indefinitely, then she was very much mistaken. He had ways and means at his disposal to find his missing girlfriend, especially one as good-looking and notice-able as Tara. In fact, he had one of two choices. He could hire a private investigator to find her, or he could spend a small fortune another way and hope-fully come up with a quicker solution.

Max decided on this latter way.

Leaning forward, he gave the taxi driver a different address from the Regency Royale, after which he set-tled back and started working out what he would say to Tara when they finally came face to face.

Two hours later—they'd hit plenty of traffic on the way back to the city—Max was in his penthouse at the hotel. Snatching up some casual clothes, he headed straight for the shower. Once refreshed and dressed in crisp cream trousers and a blue yachting top, he headed for the lift again. Thankfully, Joyce had fed him as they'd talked, so he didn't need to order any food from Room Service. It crossed his mind to make himself some coffee, but decided he didn't want to wait. Having made up his mind what other things he had to do that day, Max wasn't about to dilly-dally. If he had one virtue—Joyce didn't seem to think he had too many—it was decisiveness.

This time he called for his own car, and within minutes was driving east of the city. Thankfully, by then, the traffic was lighter. It was just after eleven-thirty, the sun was well up in the summer sky and Max would have rather gone anywhere than where he was going.

His stomach knotted as he approached his parents' home. He hadn't been to see them since Christmas, a token visit which he felt he couldn't avoid. Ever since Stevie's death, he'd kept his visits to a minimum. They were always a strain, even more so since his father's stroke. The accusing, angry words he might have once spoken—and which might have cleared the air between father and son—were always held back. He could hardly bear to watch his mother, either. He resented the way she tended to his father. So patiently, with never a cross word.

Maybe Tara was right. Maybe she really did love the man. She'd certainly been prepared to forgive him for lots of things.

Max wondered if he could ever really forgive his father. He doubted it. But he'd have to pretend to, if he was to have any chance of convincing Tara he was man enough to be a good father to their baby.

Max parked his car at the kerb outside his parents' Point Piper mansion and just sat there for a minute or two, looking at the place. It was certainly a far cry from Tara's house. Aside from the house, which ran over three levels, there were the perfectly manicured gardens at the front, a huge solar-heated pool out the back and magnificent harbour views from most of the rooms.

It was a home fit for a king. Or a prince.

He'd been brought up here, taking it all for granted. The perfect house. The private schools. Membership of the nearby yacht club.

And then there were the women. The ones who'd targeted him from the moment he'd been old enough to have sex. The ones who'd done anything and everything to get him to fall in love with them.

But he hadn't loved any of them.

The only woman he'd ever fallen for was Tara.

And she was in danger of slipping away from him, if he wasn't careful.

With his stomach still in knots, Max climbed out from behind the wheel and went inside. He still had keys. He hadn't moved out of home till after the episode with Stevie.

His mother was sitting out on the top terrace, reading the newspaper to his father, who was in his wheelchair beside her. Dressed in pale blue trousers and a pretty floral top, she was immaculately groomed as usual. Her streaked blonde hair was cut short in a modern style and she was wearing make-up and pearl earrings.

For as long as Max could remember, she'd looked much younger than her age, but today, in the harsh sunlight, she looked every one of her fifty-nine years. And then some.

Her father's appearance, however, shocked him more than his mother's. Before his stroke he'd been a vibrant, handsome man with a fit, powerful body and thick head of dark hair. Now his hair was white, his muscles withered, his skin deeply lined. He looked eighty, yet he was only sixty-two.

For the first time, some sympathy stirred in Max's

soul. Plus a measure of guilt. How come he hadn't noticed the extent of his father's deterioration at Christmas? It had only been a couple of months ago.

Maybe he hadn't noticed because he hadn't wanted to. It was easier to cling to old resentments rather than see that his father was going downhill at a rate of knots, or that his mother might need some hands-on help. Much easier to hate than to love.

Max realised in that defining moment that he didn't really hate his parents. He never had. He just didn't understand them. Tara was right when she'd said people never knew what went on in a marriage.

One thing Max did know, however, as he watched his mother reach out to tenderly touch his father's arm. She did love the man. And if the way his father looked back was any judge, then that love was returned.

Max's heart turned over as he hoped that Tara would always look at him like that.

Neither of them had seen him yet, standing there just inside the sliding glass doors which led out onto the terrace. When he slid one back, his mother's head jerked up and around, her blue eyes widening with surprise, and then pleasure.

'Max!' she exclaimed. 'Ronald, it's Max.'

'Max...' His father's hands fumbled as they reached to swivel his chair around. His eyes, too, mirrored surprise. But they were tired eyes, Max thought. Dead eyes.

All the life had gone out of him.

'Max,' the old man repeated as though he could still not believe his son had come to visit.

'Hi there, Mum. Dad,' he said as he came forward and bent to kiss his mother on the cheek. 'You're both looking well,' he added as he pulled up a chair.

His father croaked out a dry laugh. 'I look terrible and I know it.'

Max smiled a wry smile. The old man wasn't quite dead yet.

'You know, Dad, when I was a boy you told me that God helps those who help themselves. You obviously practised what you preached all your life. After all, you worked your way up from a valet-parking attendant to being one of Australia's most successful hotel owners.'

Max generously refrained from reminding his father that marrying the daughter of an established hotel baron had been a leg-up, especially when Max's maternal grandfather was already at death's door. Within weeks of Max's grandfather dying, Ronald Richmond had sold off the hotels that didn't live up to his ideals and started up the Royale chain. He hadn't looked back, till three years ago, when his stroke had forced his premature retirement.

'I have to say I'm a bit disappointed,' Max went on, 'that you seem to have thrown in the towel this time. Frankly, I expected more from you than this.'

Some more fire sparked in the old man's eyes, which was exactly what Max had intended.

'What would you know about it, boy? My whole right side is virtually useless.'

'Something which could be remedied with therapy. You should be thankful that your speech wasn't affected. Some people can't talk after a stroke.'

'My eyes are bad,' he grumbled. 'Your mother has to read to me.'

'But you're not blind. Look, how about I line up a top physiotherapist to come in every day and work with you? He'll have you up and out of that wheel-chair in no time.'

'That would be wonderful, Max,' his mother said. 'Wouldn't it, Ronald?'

'It's too late,' his father muttered. 'I'm done for.'

'Rubbish!' Max countered. 'Never too late. That's another of your own philosophies, might I remind you? Besides, I need you up and about in time for my wedding.'

'Your wedding!' they chorused, their expressions shocked.

'Yep. I'm getting married.'

After that, Max was regaled with questions. He thought he lied very well, telling them all about Tara and the baby, but nothing about her disappearance. He made it sound like a done deal that he and Tara would walk down the aisle in the near future. He also promised to bring her over to meet them by the end of the weekend. He made some excuse that she was away visiting friends for the next couple of days.

Talk about optimism!

Over lunch he also told his father that he planned to stay in Australia more in future and delegate some of the overseas travelling to his assistant.

'Good idea,' his father said, nodding. 'When a man has a family, he should not be away from home too much. I was away from home too much. Far too much.'

When tears suddenly welled up in his father's eyes, his mother immediately jumped up. 'I think it's time for your afternoon nap, dear,' she said. 'He gets tired very easily these days,' she directed at a shocked Max as she wheeled his father off. 'I won't be long. Have another cup of coffee.'

Max did just that, sitting there, sipping some coffee and doing some serious thinking till his mother returned.

She threw Max an odd look as she sat down. 'I'm so glad you stayed. Usually, you bolt out the door as soon as you can. Your becoming a father yourself has changed you, Max. You're different today. Softer. And more compassionate. Perhaps the time is right for me to tell you the truth about Stevie.'

Max stiffened. 'What...what do you mean...the truth?'

His mother heaved a deep sigh, her eyes not quite meeting his. 'Stevie was not your father's child.'

Max gaped.

'I thought you might have guessed,' she went on when he said nothing. 'After all, Stevie was very different from you. And from your father. He also had brown eyes. Two blue-eyed parents can't have a brown-eyed child, you know.'

Max shook his head. 'I didn't know that. Did Stevie?'

'Thankfully, no. At least…he never said he did.'

'So that's why Dad didn't love him.'

'You're wrong, Max. Your father did love Stevie. The trouble was every time he looked at him, he was reminded of the fact that I had slept with another man.'

'But I thought Dad was the unfaithful one!'

His mother stared at him. 'Why do you say that?'

'Years ago, I overheard you telling a friend that you knew Dad had other women, but you just turned a blind eye.'

His mother looked so sad. 'I'm so sorry you heard that. You must have thought me very weak. Or very wicked.'

'I didn't know what to think. I've never known what to think about you two. At least I can now understand why Dad treated Stevie differently from me.'

'He did try, Max. But it was very hard on him. He never seemed to know what to say to Stevie. Or how to act with him. It was much easier with you, because you were like two peas in a pod. But that didn't mean he didn't care about Stevie. When he was diagnosed with cancer, your father was terribly upset. His way of coping with his grief was to work harder. He couldn't bear to see the boy in pain. He knows now that he should have come home to be with Stevie. He understands what it's like when the people you love aren't there for you when you're ill.'

She didn't look at him directly. Neither were her words said in an accusing tone. But Max felt guilty all the same. He hadn't been any better than his father, had he? He'd let both his parents down by not being here to help.

'Your father feels his stroke was a punishment for his letting Stevie down,' his mother choked out.

Max could not deny that he had entertained similar thoughts himself over the past three years. Suddenly, however, they seemed terribly mean-spirited, and very immature. But he could not find the right words to say and was sitting there in an awkward silence, when his mother spoke once more.

'Do you want to know about Stevie's real father, or not?'

'Yes,' Max said sincerely. 'Yes, I do.'

'I have to go back to the beginning of my relationship with your father so that you can get the full picture.'

'OK.'

She smiled a wry smile. 'I hope you won't be too shocked at me.'

Max could not imagine that anything more his mother could say today would shock him.

'I'm no saint myself, Mum,' he reassured, and so she began her story.

She'd first met his father when he parked her car for her one day at one of her own father's hotels.

She'd fallen in love with him at first sight, and had pursued him shamelessly as only a spoiled and beautiful rich woman could do. She confessed to seducing him with sex and playing to his ambitious nature with her money and her contacts. Not to mention her potential fortune. She was her wealthy father's only child.

The trouble was she'd never believed he truly loved her when he married her, and was always besieged by doubts. The arrival of their first-born son—Max himself—calmed her for a while. Her husband seemed besotted, if not with her then definitely with his child. She began to feel more secure in her marriage. But after her father died and her husband started travelling overseas more and more often, all her doubts over his love increased. There was a photograph in a newspaper of him with some gorgeous socialite in London. She flew into a jealous rage when her husband finally came home, accusing him of being unfaithful. He claimed he wasn't but she didn't believe him.

Their marriage entered one of those dangerous phases. Ronald started staying away even more and she started going out on her own. She met Stevie's father at an art exhibition. *His* art exhibition. He was an up-and-coming artist. She'd argued with her husband over the phone earlier in the evening over his delaying his return home yet again and was in a reckless mood. She drank too much and the rest, as they said, was history.

Perversely, Ronald arrived home the next night, and when she discovered she was pregnant a month later she didn't know whose baby she was having. When the baby was born with blue eyes, she thought Stevie was Max's full brother. But by six months his eyes had changed to brown and he looked nothing like Max's father.

When Ronald confronted her with his suspicions, she confessed her indiscretion and her husband went crazy, showing her at last that he did love her. But the marriage had been irreparably damaged. After that, she suspected her husband was no longer faithful to her when he went away. A few times, she found evidence of other women on his clothes. Lipstick and perfume. She turned a blind eye for fear that he might actually divorce her. She tried to make a life for herself with charity work and society functions but she was very unhappy.

She reiterated that when Stevie was diagnosed with cancer, Ronald *had* been genuinely upset. Unfortunately, his way of handling such an emotional crisis was to go into his cave, so to speak, and work harder than ever.

'Stevie might have survived his sickness,' his mother added, 'if it hadn't been for his girlfriend dumping him. That was what depressed him far more than his father not being around. Trust me on that. Stevie and I were very close and he told me everything he felt.'

Max nodded. 'I can imagine. I've never known a

boy like Stevie. The way he could express his feelings. I wish I could be like that sometimes.'

'His biological father was like that,' his mother said. 'A real talker. And a deep thinker. A sweet, soft, sensitive man whom you couldn't help liking. He made me feel so special that night. He didn't know I was married, of course. He was shocked when I told him afterwards. Didn't want anything more to do with me. As I said, a nice man.'

'I see. So he never knew about Stevie?'

'God, no. No, I never saw him again. Sadly, he died a few years later. Cancer. And they say it's not hereditary…'

Tears glistened in her eyes as she looked straight at Max. 'Your father finally forgave me. But can you?'

Not ever being at his best with words, Max stood up and came round to bend and kiss his mother on the cheek.

Her hands lifted to cover his, which had come to rest on her shoulders. She patted them, then glanced up at him. 'Thank you. You're a good boy, Max. But a terrible liar. Now, why don't you sit back down and tell *me* the total truth about this girl of yours? I'd especially like to know how someone as clever as you could have made the mistake of making her pregnant in the first place. Or was that *her* idea? You are a very rich man, after all.'

Max walked back to settle in his chair before answering.

'I have to confess that idea did briefly occur to me. But only briefly. You'll see when you meet Tara that she does not have a greedy, or a manipulative bone in her body.'

'Tara,' his mother said. 'Such a lovely name.'

'She's a lovely girl.'

'And was it her idea for you to come here today?'

'Not directly. But she would have approved. The fact is, Mum, I don't know where Tara is. She's run away.'

'Run away! Max, whatever did you do?'

'It's what I *didn't* do which caused the problem. When she told me she was having a baby, I didn't tell her I loved her. And I didn't ask her to marry me.'

'Oh, Max... No wonder she ran away. She must be heartbroken.'

'Don't say that, Mum,' he said with a tightening in his chest. 'I don't want to hear that. I'm just hanging in here as it is, waiting for tomorrow.'

'What's going to happen tomorrow?'

He told her.

CHAPTER ELEVEN

TARA lay in bed, slowly nibbling on one of the dry biscuits she'd put beside the bed the night before. Hopefully, they would make her feel well enough to rise shortly and go for a walk on the beach.

Yesterday, she'd stayed in bed most of the day before going for a walk. But then yesterday she'd been desperately tired.

Today she'd woken more refreshed, but still nauseous. Hence the biscuits.

It had been good of Kate to give her some, no questions asked. Although there'd been a slight speculative gleam in her eyes as she'd handed Tara the plate of biscuits after dinner last night.

But that was Kate all over. The woman was kind and accommodating without being a sticky-beak, all good qualities for anyone who ran a bed and breakfast establishment. Tara had met her a few years ago when she'd stayed here at Kate's Place with some of her uni friends. It was popular with students because it had been cheap and conveniently located, only a short stroll to Wamberal Beach.

When she'd been thinking of where she could go and be by herself for a while, Tara had immediately thought of Kate's Place. Wamberal was not far away from Sydney—an hour and a half's drive north—but far enough away that she would feel secure that she wouldn't run into Max, or anyone who knew Max.

So on Thursday night she'd taken a taxi to Hornsby railway station, then a train to Gosford, then another taxi to Wamberal Beach. Rather naively, in a way. What would she have done if Kate had sold the place in the years since she'd stayed there? Or if she didn't have any spare rooms to rent?

Fate had been on her side this time and whilst Kate had gone more upmarket—renaming her refurbished home Kate's Beachside B & B—she had still been in the room-renting business, although the number of rooms available had been reduced to three.

Fortunately, all of them were vacant. The end of February, whilst still summer, was not peak tourist season. On top of that she'd stopped advertising, not wanting to be full all of the time.

'I'm getting old,' she'd complained as she showed Tara upstairs. 'But I'd be bored if I stopped having people to stay altogether. And terribly lonely. Still, I might have to give it away when I turn seventy next year. Or give in and hire a cleaner.'

Tara had selected the bedroom at the front of the two-storeyed home, which had a lovely view of the beach as well as an *en suite* bathroom. No way did she want to have to race down hallways to a communal bathroom first thing in the morning.

True to form, Kate hadn't asked her any questions on her arrival, although Tara had spotted some concern in the elderly woman's eyes. She supposed it was rare for a guest to show up, unannounced and un-booked, at ten-thirty at night. Tara's excuse that it was a spur-of-the-moment impulse had probably not been believed.

But Kate at least appreciated that she was an adult with the right to come and go as she pleased, some-thing Tara wished other people recognised. She was not a child who had to be directed. She did have a mind of her own and she was quite capable of making decisions, provided she was given the time to work out what was best for herself, and the baby.

Impossible to even think at home at the moment with her mother criticising and nagging all the time. Jen wasn't much better. She seemed to have forgotten how emotional and irrational *she* was when she found out she was pregnant.

Of course, Tara would not have bolted quite so melodramatically if Max hadn't been on his way. Max of the 'we should work this out together' mode.

Huh! Tara knew what that meant. Max, taking total control and telling her what to do.

From what she'd seen, Max had no idea how to truly work together with anyone or anything. Max ordered and people obeyed.

She'd been obeying him for twelve months.

But not any more.

The time had come for mutiny.

Her first step had been to put herself beyond his reach. Which she had. And, to be honest, taking that action had felt darned good. Clearly, she'd been harbouring more resentment than she realised over Max's dominant role in their relationship.

Not so good was the niggling remorse she felt over her mother. By last night guilt had begun to override her desperate need for peace and privacy. She would have to ring her mother today. It wasn't fair to leave her worrying.

And she would be worrying. Tara had no doubt of that.

A firm tap-tap on her bedroom door had Tara calling out that she was coming before gingerly swinging her feet onto the floor and standing up. As she reached for the silky housecoat she'd brought with her, she was pleased to find her stomach hadn't heaved at all when she got to her feet. Those biscuits seemed to have done the trick.

But still, she didn't hurry, taking her time as she padded across the floral rug which covered most of the polished floorboards. Kate's décor leant towards old world, but Tara liked it.

She opened the door to find Kate standing there with a newspaper in her hands and a worried look on her face.

'Yes?' Tara asked.

Kate didn't say a word. She just handed the newspaper to Tara. It was opened and folded back at page three.

Tara went cold all over as she stared down at the full-page photograph of herself, an enlargement of the one she knew Max kept in his wallet. It had been taken on one of their first dinner dates, at a restaurant where a photographer went around and snapped photos of people who were likely to buy them as mementos. Targeted were groups partying there for special occasions, plus romantic couples possibly celebrating their engagements, or just their love for each other.

Tara could see the happiness shining out of her eyes in that photograph. She doubted her eyes would reflect the same emotion at that moment.

Her teeth clenched hard in her jaw as she glared down at the words written across the bottom of the photograph.

Tara, your loved ones are worried about you. Please call home. If anyone knows Tara's whereabouts, contact the following number for a substantial reward.

Tara's head shot up. 'Please don't tell me you rang it. That's not my home phone number. It belongs to my boyfriend.'

'Not me, love. But Milly Jenson did. My busybody neighbour. She must have had a good look at you when you went out walking yesterday afternoon. I think her conscience finally got the better of her and she came and told me what she'd done. Either that, or she was indulging in more mischief-making. Either way, I thought you'd want to know.'

'I certainly do. Thanks, Kate,' she said, her head whirling with the news Max was on his way up here.

'Boyfriend, eh? Not one you'll be wanting to see again, I'll warrant. Do you want me to drive you anywhere, love? I can get you away from here before he arrives. Milly gave him this address over an hour ago, so he could be arriving any time soon.'

Tara thought about running away again, then decided there was little point. Wherever she went, someone would spot her and call Max and that would be that. Her stand-out looks had always been a curse. Oh, how she would have preferred to be less striking. Less tall. Less blonde!

She shook her head as she stared down again at the photograph in the paper.

'Thank you, Kate, but no. I'll talk to him when he arrives. But not here. I have no intention of meekly staying here till he arrives. I'll get dressed right now and go for a walk on the beach. You can point him in that direction when he arrives. OK?'

'Only OK if he's no danger to you, love. He hasn't been beating you up, has he?'

'Good lord, no! Max would never do anything like that. But as you might have gathered he's very rich. And used to getting his own way. He's also the father of my baby. I'm pregnant, Kate.'

'Yes, so I gathered, love. That's a popular old remedy, eating dry biscuits when you're suffering from morning sickness. As soon as you asked me for them, I guessed.'

'You didn't say anything.'

'Not my place. I keep my nose out of other people's private business. Except when it comes to arrogant members of the opposite sex. One of the reasons I never married was because I couldn't stand it when men thought they could run my life. Oh, yes, I had quite a few suitors when I was younger. All wanting me to marry them, especially the ones I slept with. One became very insistent once he found out I was having his baby. More than insistent. Violent, actually. As if I would ever marry a man who hit me. Or inflict such a father on an innocent child.'

Tara's mouth had dropped open slightly at these astonishing revelations. But it seemed Kate was not yet finished baring her soul, or her rather adventurous past.

'If it had been more acceptable back in my day, I would have chosen to be a single mother. But I didn't. I did something else, love, something I've always bitterly regretted. Girls these days have so many options. So don't do what I did, love. You have your baby and to hell with what this man says or wants. He can't be much of a man if you ran away from him like that.'

'He's not a bad man,' Tara said. 'Or a violent one. He's just…domineering.'

'Does he want you to have an abortion?'

'I don't know.'

'Mmm… Does he love you?'

She frowned down at the photograph, then nodded.

'Yes. I think he does. As much as he is capable of loving.'

'He sounds a bit mixed up.'

'You know what, Kate, I think he is. Yet he's very successful. And filthy rich.'

'And wickedly handsome, no doubt,' Kate said drily.

'Oh, yes. That too.'

Kate pulled a face. 'They always are. I'll see what I think of him when he arrives, then I'll put him through the third degree before I tell him where you've gone. Would you mind if I did that?'

Tara had to laugh. 'Not at all. Do him good.'

'Right. You hurry and get yourself dressed now. And take one of the sunhats from off the pegs by the front door. Put your hair up under it. And pop some sunglasses on. Otherwise you'll have everyone on the beach who's seen this photograph in this morning's paper running home to call that number.'

'I'll do that. And Kate...'

'Yes?'

'Thank you. You've been very kind. And wonderfully understanding.'

Kate smiled a surprisingly mischievous smile. 'We girls have to stick together.'

Max stomped over the sand, disbelieving of what that woman had just put him through before telling him where Tara was. Anyone would think he was a murderer instead of a man in love, trying to do the right thing!

His gaze scanned the various semi-naked bodies sprawled over the warm sand. None of them was Tara. He would recognise her in a heartbeat. He headed for the water's edge and stood there, searching for her tell-tale head of fair hair amongst the swimmers. Not there, either.

A rogue wave suddenly washed further up the beach than the others, totally soaking his expensive Italian loafers.

Max swore.

Still, ruining a pair of shoes was the least of his worries at that moment. Where was Tara? Had that old tartar lied to him? Was Tara at this very moment on her way somewhere else?

Max's stomach began to churn. And then he saw her, further down the wide arch of beach, paddling along the water's edge, coming towards him.

It wasn't her hair which revealed her identity. Her long blonde mane was out of sight underneath a large straw hat. It was her legs which gave her away. Not many girls had legs like Tara's.

She was wearing shorts. Denim, with frayed edges. And a red singlet top. No bra, he noticed as she drew closer.

The automatic stirring of his body annoyed him. This was not why he had come. Tara already knew he wanted her sexually. He had to convince her that he wanted her for much more than that.

Willing his flesh back under control, he marched towards her, determined not to let desire distract him. For he suspected if it did, he was doomed to failure. And failure was not something Max could cope with today. His mission was to win Tara back, not lose her. Instinct warned him that making love to her in any way, shape or form would lose her for sure. His job was to convince her that he would make a good husband and father, not just a good lover.

Tara had spotted Max some time back, but she gave no signal to him, watching surreptitiously as he'd made his way with some difficulty across the soft sand. He was hardly dressed for the beach in grey dress trousers and a long-sleeved white silk shirt, even though the shirt *was* rolled up at the sleeves and left open at the neck.

It had amused her when the wave washed over his shoes. She wasn't so amused now as he hurried towards her. Most annoying was the way her body went into full foreplay mode at his approach. Her heartbeat quickened. Her nipples hardened. Her belly tightened. All in anticipation of his touch.

Disgusting, she thought. Deplorable!

Delicious, another darker, more devilish part of her brain whispered.

She sighed. Clearly, she still had to be careful with him. Her sexual vulnerability remained high.

Of course, if this was a romantic movie, both of them would suddenly break into a run and throw themselves into each other's arms. They would kiss, the music would soar and THE END would come up on the screen.

But this was not a movie. It was real life with real people and real issues. Serious relationship problems were never solved with one kiss. Making love was a masking agent, not a lasting solution.

No way was she going to let him touch her. Not today, anyway.

'Max,' she said drily when he was close enough.

Thankfully, he ground to a halt outside of grabbing and kissing distance. Though was it Max doing that which worried her the most? Or her own silly self?

'So you found me,' she added, and crossed her arms. Not only did the action demonstrate he wasn't all that welcome, but it also hid her infernal nipples.

'With some difficulty,' came his sharp return.

Clearly, he was not in a good mood. Kate must have given him heaps. But not as much as *she* was going to give him.

'I don't know how you can say that. One little— or should I say not so little?—photograph in the paper, with the added incentive of a reward, and Bob's your uncle, you had your man.'

His gaze ran down her body then up again. 'No one in their wildest dreams, Tara, would call you a man.'

Tara pulled a face at him. 'You know, it must be wonderful to have enough money to buy anything you want.'

His eyes searched hers, as though he was weighing up her attitude. Her sarcastic tone had to be telling him something.

'You're still angry with me,' he said. 'And you have every right to be. I didn't handle your news the other night at all well.'

'No. You certainly didn't.'

'There again, you didn't give me much opportunity to make things right by hanging up on me and then running away. That was hardly fair, Tara. Even you have to agree your news was a shock. I was not prepared for it.'

'Tough. I did what I had to do. For me.'

'And have you come to any decisions during your time alone?'

'Would you mind if we walk while we talk?'

Tara just started walking, forcing him to fall into step beside her.

'I'd prefer to go sit somewhere private together.'

I'll just bet you would, she thought ruefully. Before she knew it he would be kissing her and she'd either go to mush, or hit him. Neither prospect pleased her. This was her chance to show him that she would not live her life on *his* terms. Seeing him in the flesh again, however, had brought home to her that he still wielded great power over her. She had to be very careful. And very strong.

'I'm hardly dressed for the beach, Tara,' he pointed out. 'I'm ruining my shoes for starters.'

'You chose to come up here, Max. I didn't make

you. Take off your shoes, if you're worried about them. And roll up your trousers.'

To her astonishment, he did just that. Unfortunately, it made her even more physically aware of him. Being pregnant didn't seem to have dampened her desires one iota. If anything, she craved Max's lovemaking even more. How contrary could you get?

'I called your mother,' he said when they started walking again. 'Told her I'd found you. Joyce said to tell you to believe me when I say that I would never have tried to talk you into an abortion.'

Any relief Tara felt over this news was overshadowed by shock, and anger. She ground to a halt and spun in the sand to face him.

'*Joyce?* Since when did you call my mother *Joyce*? And since when has she started taking *your* side?'

'Since we had a good chat yesterday morning.'

Tara laughed. A dry, knowing laugh. 'I get it. You told Mum you were prepared to marry me and she melted. That's the be-all and end-all with Mum. Marriage.'

'You make it sound like a crime.'

'It is if you marry for all the wrong reasons.'

'You think my loving you is a wrong reason?'

Tara found it increasingly difficult to hold her temper. 'You've told me you love me. But not one mention of marriage. So why now? As if I don't know. You've decided you want your child. You're getting older and it's suddenly come home to you that maybe an heir in your image and likeness would be a very nice thing to have, along with a silly, besotted wife who thinks the sun shines out of your bum and who'll wait around for you for weeks at a time, no questions asked.'

'Now wait a minute!'

'No, *you* wait a minute. It's your turn to do the waiting, buster.'

An angry colour slanted across his cheekbones, and his hands tightened their grip on his shoes.

But he stayed tactfully silent, allowing her the opportunity to say what was on her mind. And there was plenty!

'You must have thought you were on to a good thing this past year. You never explained and I never complained. Of course, things weren't absolutely perfect for you. Whilst I'm sure it was exciting and ego-stroking at first to have a virgin in your bed—something tells me you hadn't had the pleasure of one of *those* before!—I didn't quite have the confidence you would have liked. Till last weekend. After which, suddenly, I was being invited to travel with you.'

'That's not true!' he protested.

'Of course it's true! I've finally grown up, Max. I don't see you through rose-coloured glasses any more. I can even appreciate your reasoning. Why go to the trouble of finding suitable one-night stands in whatever city you were in, when you could take the new me with you for the price of a plane ticket?'

She saw his eyes darken, but she hadn't finished.

'Even better was the fact that I had the makings of such a *cheap* mistress. A dress here and there. The odd outing. Some champagne and you'd be In Like Flynn.'

'Now, hold it right there!' he ground out. 'Firstly, I was never unfaithful to you. Not once. Secondly, I never thought of you as my mistress. I always meant to marry you, Tara. When the time was right.'

'Really? And when would that have been?'

'When I was less busy and you were older. My asking you to travel with me was a compromise. I was afraid of losing you. Just as I'm afraid of losing you now. Losing you and our baby.'

It shocked Tara, his admitting to such emotions. Max, the macho man, was not given to admitting that he was afraid of losing anything. But then she realised his confessing such fears was his way of *not* losing. His words were designed to weaken her resolve, to make her do what *he* wanted, as usual.

'I love you, Tara,' he went on. 'I've loved you from the beginning. I know I told you I didn't want marriage and children, and I meant it at the time. But things have changed. You're going to have my baby.'

'Yes, Max, I am. And yes, things have changed. But you haven't. You're still the same Max I met. The same exciting, successful, ambitious, ruthless man. Just look at what you did to find me. What kind of man does something like that?'

'The kind you fell in love with. But you're wrong, Tara. I *can* change. I've already started.'

'How? I see no evidence of it.'

'Come back to Sydney with me and I'll show you.'

'No.'

His head jerked back, blue eyes shocked. 'No?'

'No. That's part of your problem, Max. People jump to do your bidding far too much. I've been way too accommodating where you're concerned. I've always done what you wanted. Now you can do what *I* want for a change.'

'Tell me and I'll do it,' he stated boldly.

And rather recklessly, Tara thought. No way would he agree to what she was about to demand. But it would be interesting to see how he tried to wriggle out of it.

'All right. Go home, collect some beach clothes and come back up here. Kate will rent you a room. Stay here, with me, for a week. Separate rooms. No sex. We'll spend quality time together, but we'll just talk.'

Tara was quietly confident he would never just drop his business commitments like that.

'It's a deal,' he said.

Tara blinked in shock, but reserved her judgement till he actually followed through.

'What happens at the end of the week?' he asked.

'I'll let you know...at the end of the week.'

'That doesn't seem fair.'

'I'm not going to explain and you're not to complain. You are just to do what I want, when I want.'

'But no sex.'

'Absolutely no sex.'

'Mmm. Are you sure you can handle that?'

Her chin lifted. 'No trouble,' she lied.

'I will only agree to those conditions if, at the end of the week, I get to take you out to dinner, then back to bed for the night. The whole night. In the same bed.'

'Why does there have to be a catch?'

'Darling, there's always a catch. There's no such thing as a free lunch, or a free week of total slavery and submission. Which is what you're asking for. I know you want me to prove to you that I love you. That I don't want you just for sex. Fine. I'm happy to do that. But then I want the chance to show you that I do love you. *My* way.'

Tara's heart turned over. She knew, once she was in his arms again, that all her new resolves would weaken. She had one week to achieve all she wanted to achieve. One week to make Max see that the only way they could be truly happy was if he offered her a genuine partnership, not just a ring on her finger.

'You sure have developed a way with words all of a sudden,' she tossed back at him. 'We'll see if you can keep it up for a week.'

He laughed. 'I'll have no trouble keeping it up. Especially if you go round looking like that all the time.'

Tara flushed. 'If you try to seduce me, Max, you'll be sorry.'

'You don't know who you're talking to, honey.

This is the boy who went for three days without food. Going without sex couldn't be as hard as that. Oops. Scratch that word hard and replace it with difficult.'

Tara frowned at him. This was the first time he'd spoken of himself when he was a boy. That was something she would get him to do during the next week. Open up to her about his childhood. Intimacy was not just about sex, but also about knowing all there was to know about your partner.

'Why did you go without food?'

'Mum was raising funds for some charity. She spent half her life doing that. This time, she got us kids involved. Stevie found sponsors who paid various amounts for his reading books. I think he read eighty-five books. I chose to starve. Got paid a fortune for every day I went without food. Much easier than reading. I hate reading.'

'Nothing's changed in that regard,' Tara said drily. 'You don't have any decent books at the penthouse. Just boring stuff about business and sport. You don't know what you're missing, Max. Reading is a fabulous past-time. I'll read you some good books this week whilst we lie on the beach. Kate has a wonderful selection of best-sellers.'

Max winced.

'Having second thoughts already?' Tara said in a challenging tone.

'Definitely not,' he replied. And smiled.

Tara wasn't sure she liked that smile. There was something sneaky about it.

'I'd better get going if I'm to get back today,' he said.

'You only have to pack a few clothes.'

'And make a few phone calls. I have to let Pierce know where I'll be, for one thing.'

'If you take or make one business phone call during your week up here, Max, the deal's off.'

Max suspected she was bluffing, but he had to admire her stance. Tara didn't realise it but he would never marry a mealy-mouthed woman, or one who kow-towed to him all the time. Most of his life, he'd been pursued by women who indulged his every desire, in bed and out of it. He liked it that Tara was finally standing up to him; that she was so strong. She was going to make a wonderful wife and mother.

His eyes softened on her. 'Fair enough. I'll leave my mobile at home.' With his father. Do the old man good to have to make some business decisions. Probably perk him up no end. But not as much as that physio he'd hired yesterday to come in every day and work those atrophied muscles. Max had stayed with his parents all day Friday, inspiring both of them with their new role as grandparents-to-be, leaving them looking younger than when he arrived. 'I'll be back before you can say Jack Robinson.'

'Don't speed,' she warned him. 'I'd like our child to have a live father, not a memorial in some ceme-tery.'

'Right. No speeding. Any other instructions? Or rules?'

Her head tipped to one side and her lips pursed.

God, how he would love to just slide his hands around that lovely long neck of hers and kiss that luscious mouth till it was soft and malleable. Till *she* was soft and malleable.

Instead, he had to stand there and play at being a sensitive, new-age guy. Not a role Max aspired to. He had definite ideas about male roles in life, and wishy-washy wimp was not one of them. He could not wait for this week to be over. Already he was looking forward to the following Saturday night.

'None that I can think of at the moment,' she said. 'But I'll have a written list by the time you return.'

Max blinked. My God, she meant it. Maybe he shouldn't marry her at all. Strong, he liked. But a bossy-boots nag was another story.

What she needed, of course, was a night in bed. With him. Those rock-like nipples said something else to the words coming out of her mouth. By the time this week was up, he wouldn't be the only one having cold showers.

But he could be patient, if the rewards were worth it. What better reward could there be than to have Tara back in his arms once more, right where she belonged?

CHAPTER TWELVE

A WEEK was a long time in politics. Or so they said. Probably because of the great changes which could happen in such a relatively short space of time.

When Max looked back over the past seven days he marvelled at the changes which had taken place, mostly within himself.

The tanned man jogging down to the beach at dawn this morning with a surfboard tucked under his arm was not the same man who'd arrogantly thought of his deal with Tara as an endurance test, to be tolerated but not enjoyed. A means to an end. A pain in the neck, as well as in other parts of his body.

Max had not anticipated the delights, or the discoveries he had made during the past week.

Tara had been so right in forbidding all business calls, for starters. He hadn't realised just how much of every day he spent on work and work-related issues. He'd actually suffered withdrawal symptoms at first. But soon, he wasn't giving a thought to whether profits were up or down. Neither did he worry over what new worldwide crisis might happen which would impact on the hotel industry.

No news was definitely good news.

After a few days he'd even revised his earlier decision to just delegate more in future so that he would have more time for Tara and their child. Now he was thinking of downsizing the Royale chain of hotels altogether. Travelling all over the world and spending every day in meetings or having business dinners no longer held such an attraction for him.

Max plunged into the surf, deftly sliding his body face-down onto the board as he hand-paddled out across the waves. The sun had just broken over the horizon, the blue-green sea sparkling under its rays. Once out into deeper water, Max sat up and straddled the board, watching and waiting for just the right wave to ride in.

This was good!

He'd forgotten how much he'd liked surfing. He hadn't done any in years. But when Kate offered him use of the spare surfboards and wetsuits she kept in the garage, he couldn't resist. And, after a few minor disasters, he'd regained his balance, his confidence and his natural athletic skill. Max had been born good at all sports.

Each morning since, he'd spent a few hours in the surf whilst Tara languished in bed. She was still not feeling tippy-top in the mornings. By eleven she would be up and he would return for a shower and a leisurely brunch. Kate was an excellent if old-fashioned cook, paying no mind to the modern dictates of low-fat food. Max might have put on quite a few pounds if he hadn't been using up a few thousand calories each day in the water. Tara was saved by her delicate stomach, keeping to tea and toast.

After brunch, he and Tara would take a beach umbrella and a book, find a nice spot on the side of one of the sand dunes which overlooked the ocean and settle down to read. The first time they'd done this, Max had thought he would have to pretend to enjoy being read to. But Tara was such an expressive reader, and the best-seller she chose to read obviously hadn't been a best-seller for nothing. It was one of those legal thrillers which twisted and turned on every page. The murder trial itself had been riveting. He'd changed his mind on who the killer was several times but finally settled on the wife, and had been tickled pink when he was proved right.

His remark to Tara during one of these early reading sessions that his mother read to his father these days had led to his finally telling her about his reconciliation with his parents. He'd talked to Tara for ages over dinner that night about his parents' marriage and all their misunderstandings. In fact, this past week, he'd talked more about his parents and his growing-up years than he ever had in his life.

Admittedly, there wasn't much else he could do but talk to Tara. She hadn't wavered from her strictly hands-off rule the whole week. Not an easy situation to bear with her going round in an itsy-bitsy bikini most of the time. In the end, he'd ordered that she cover up when she wasn't swimming, mostly for his own frustration's sake but partly because he was sick to death of the ogling of other males on the beach. She'd given him a droll look and totally ignored him.

Max realised at that point that she might never obey any of his orders ever again. The jury was still out on whether he liked that idea, or not.

Still, she'd had some jealousy of her own to contend with. His own ego had been benefiting from some serious stroking with the looks he'd been getting from the local ladies, the mirror telling him that his less hectic and more outdoor lifestyle was suiting him.

He was going to hate having to give it up.

But why would you *have* to? his brain piped up. You're a very wealthy man. And a smart one. Surely you can work something out. If you downsize the hotel chain the way you're going to, the demands on your personal time will be lessened. With all the modern communication technology around, you can keep in touch with the world from anywhere. You don't even have to be in Sydney. You could be up here, in one of those houses right over there…

His gaze scanned the various buildings fronting Wamberal Beach. Some were holiday apartment blocks. Some were large homes. But some were simple and rather small beach houses, built decades ago. Surely one of those owners could be persuaded to sell. He could have it pulled down and build the home of Tara's dream, with a granny flat for Joyce.

No, no, that wouldn't work. Joyce wouldn't like to be that far away from Jen and her children. She was needed to look after the children after school on the days when Tara's sister was at work.

Max hadn't been the only one to talk this past week. Tara had told him things about her family that she hadn't told him before, possibly because he'd never asked. It was no wonder she thought he was only interested in her body.

Actions *were* louder than words.

Max's brain started ticking away. What time was it? Around seven was his best guess. He had twelve hours before he took Tara out to dinner tonight. Twelve hours before he asked her to marry him again.

He had to have more armoury than romantic words and a two-carat diamond. Flashy gifts and verbal promises wouldn't cut it with Tara. Not any more. He needed proof that he meant what he said. When he took her to bed tonight, he wanted more than his ring on her finger. He wanted her to have faith in their marriage. He wanted her trust that he would be a good husband and father.

Max's heart flipped over when he thought of that last part. He was going to become a father. An enormous responsibility. But also, hopefully, a joyful and satisfying experience. But there would be no true joy or satisfaction unless he could be a hands-on father, not a long-distance one, as his own father had been.

No, this was the place to live and bring up his son or daughter. Max resolved to make it happen, come hell or high water. The trouble was, he had to start making it happen in the next twelve hours.

So much to do, yet so little time.

It would be a challenge all right. But Max liked a challenge more than anything else.

Putting his head down, he caught the next wave to shore and started running towards Kate's place.

Tara rose earlier than usual, courtesy of the wonderful discovery that she didn't feel sick that morning. Not even a small swirl of nausea as she made her way from the bed to the bathroom.

It was a good omen, she believed.

The agreed week was over and Max was not planning to sweep her back to Sydney today, as she had feared he might. Yesterday afternoon he'd said he was happy to stay on till Sunday.

Of course, possibly that was because Kate had announced earlier at brunch that she herself was off to Sydney today for a family reunion at her niece's home, and would not be returning till Sunday morning.

Tara had no doubt Max would claim his reward tonight, either in his bed or in hers. No doubt also that once she was in his arms and vulnerable to his will, he was sure to ask her to marry him again. After a week of being with him and not being able to touch him, Tara suspected she would be extra vulnerable tonight. Her forbidding any physical contact this past week had been hard on her as well. Jen had always complained that when she was pregnant, she couldn't stand sex. It seemed with Tara it was just the opposite.

She stepped into the shower and began to lather up her hair with shampoo. But her mind was still on tonight, not her ablutions.

What would she say to Max when he proposed again? What *could* she say? He was the father of her baby, the man she loved. Her answer was probably a foregone conclusion. She knew that. She'd always known that. Her escape up here was just a temporary gesture of defiance.

Yet it had been worth it. She'd regained some control over her life and shown Max she was not a pushover, or weak. And she'd seen a side to Max which had surprised and pleased her. He *was* capable of not living and breathing his work. He was even capable of enjoying life like an ordinary, everyday person.

He loved surfing. And was surprisingly good at it. He was also learning to love books. Soon, he'd be as addicted to reading as she was. She'd also shown him that you didn't have to eat cordon bleu cuisine at five-star restaurants to enjoy eating out. Each evening, she'd insisted they go to one of the local community-based clubs where the meals were quite cheap, often buffet-style for a set price. At one place, they'd had a roast dinner—with a free glass of beer thrown in—for eight dollars each. Max had been amazed, both at the price and the reasonable quality of the food.

But had his pleasure and co-operation this past week been real, or a con?

The truth was Tara still did not totally trust Max to be the kind of husband she wanted. Or the kind of father for their baby. In the past week, her baby had become very real to her. She loved him or her already and refused to subject her precious child to a life full of neglect and insecurity. Money alone did not bring happiness.

If Max couldn't provide the kind of secure family life she wanted for her child, then she just might have to say no to any proposal of marriage. *If* she could find the courage.

It was nine o'clock before Tara made it downstairs, taking time to blow-dry her hair and put some make-up on. She found Kate in her large, cosy kitchen, sitting at her country-style wooden table, having a cup of tea.

'You're up early today,' Kate said on seeing her. 'Feeling better? I'll get you a cuppa.'

'No, don't get up,' Tara returned swiftly. 'I can get it for myself. And yes, I'm feeling much better today. Max still surfing, I presume?'

'Actually, no, he's gone.'

Tara spun round from where she'd already crossed to the kitchen counter. 'Gone? Gone where?'

'To Sydney, he said. On business. But don't worry. He promised he'd be back in plenty of time to take you out for dinner this evening.'

A huge wave of disappointment swamped Tara. 'And there I was,' she muttered, 'thinking he'd been genuinely enjoying himself surfing every morning. But I was fooling myself. And he was fooling me.'

'No, I don't think that's the case, Tara. He did go surfing early, as usual. But he came racing back here shortly after seven, saying he had some urgent things he had to do in Sydney before tonight.'

'Such as what?' she snapped.

'He didn't say.'

'No. No, he wouldn't have. That's the old Max I grew to know and love,' she said sarcastically. 'Some business brainstorm probably struck out of the blue and he was off.'

'It might not have been *business* business, Tara, but personal business. He's probably gone to Sydney to buy you an engagement ring. How could he ask you to marry him over dinner tonight without a ring?'

'Now, why didn't I think of that?' Tara said, still with a bitter edge to her voice. 'I'm sure you're right, Kate. But trust me, he'll do business business as well whilst he's there.'

'And is that so very wrong? He is responsible for running a huge chain of international hotels, Tara. It could not have been easy for him to drop everything as you asked for a whole week. I'm sure the main thing on Max's mind today is tonight. Just before he left, he asked me to book a table for two at the best restaurant around. I chose Jardines. Very romantic place overlooking Terrigal.'

Tara sighed and shook her head at Kate. 'He's won you over too, hasn't he? Charmed you, as he did my mother. And now you're doing his bidding, as he expects all women to do. God, but we're both fools.'

'I have never been a fool where men are concerned, my dear,' Kate said with steel in her voice. 'I can always see them for what they are, once I have had the time to observe them properly. I have to confess that my first impression of Max was not too favourable. But then, I had been biased by the fact that you had run away from him. I had been ready to think poorly of him. He didn't help his cause, either, by being a tad arrogant and impatient with me that first day. But I now see your Max for what he really is. Basically, a good man. A decent man. A man willing to do anything to win back the woman he loves. That is a man in a million, my dear. A man to be treasured, not hastily condemned. Wait and see what it is he's up to today before you pass judgement. I think you might be pleasantly surprised.'

Tara decided not to argue with Kate any more. No point. Kate could never know Max as well as she did. Clearly, he'd been on his best behaviour this past week, all with a purpose. Max had a mission, which was to pull the wool over both Kate's and Tara's eyes and get what he wanted. Her, back being his *yes* girl.

Max might not realise it but he'd just made a huge tactical error in going back to Sydney without even speaking to her. By falling back into his old patterns of behaviour, he'd shown her that he hadn't really changed. He was just as selfish and inconsiderate as ever.

Kate stood up and carried her cup and saucer over to load it into the dishwasher. 'I have to get going, love,' she said as she poured in some dishwashing powder then set the machine in motion. 'I'm sure Max will ring you later and explain. You wait and see.'

Tara nodded and smiled, but the moment Kate was gone she marched over to where Kate kept her phone on the wall in the kitchen and took it off the hook. If and when Max did ring, he would not get the satisfaction of a reply. He would be the one who would have to wait and see. Then, when he eventually arrived back, he was in for a big surprise!

CHAPTER THIRTEEN

MAX had been frustrated by his inability to ring Tara all day. The phone company said Kate's phone was off the hook. He tried telling himself this was probably accidental. Kate was an older lady after all. Some older ladies did things like that.

Still, it worried him. And so he hurried. As much as he could. But visiting everyone concerned and selling them on his ideas was not a quick or easy task. It took him most of the day.

Between times, he rang every real-estate agency on the central coast, making enquiries about properties for sale in Wamberal. By four that afternoon, he was back at the penthouse to freshen up and have a quick bite to eat. By four-thirty he was on the road again, heading north towards Wamberal Beach.

The tightness in his stomach became more pronounced the closer he got. Perhaps if Kate had been there with Tara, he might not have felt so agitated. Kate was on his side now. He could see that. But the dear old thing had gone to a family do, leaving Tara alone.

The possibility that Tara had deliberately taken the phone off the hook gnawed away at him. She'd done it once before, hadn't she, when she'd run away? The thought haunted him that she might not be there when he got back.

He should have knocked on her bedroom door this morning and spoken to her personally. But he hadn't wanted to disturb her. Still, he'd left a message for her with Kate, hadn't he?

Hadn't he?

Max tried to recall what he'd actually said.

Not much, he finally realised. Not *enough*.

When would he ever learn? He should have at least written her a personal note.

'Damn and blast,' he muttered, and put his foot down.

But then he remembered what Tara had said about speeding and he slowed down to the limit again.

It was just on six as he turned into Kate's place. There was no gate to open and he followed the gravel driveway round the back of the house, where there were several guest parking bays. The sun was low in the sky and the house looked quiet. Too quiet.

But the back door wasn't locked. Max heaved a huge sigh of relief...till he saw Tara's bag sitting in the front hallway.

A black pit opened up in his stomach. She was leaving.

'Tara?' he called out.

No answer. He checked the downstairs rooms, but she wasn't in any of them. He took the stairs two at a time, his heart thudding behind his ribs. She wasn't in her bedroom, or in the nearby common room, which was a combination television-sitting room with sliding glass doors that led out onto a wide upper deck.

It was there that he found her, standing at the railing, staring out towards the ocean horizon. His heart caught at how beautiful she looked, with her long blonde hair blowing back in the sea breeze and her skin a warm golden colour from their week up here. She was wearing a simple floral sun-dress with tiny straps and very little back. Fawn sandals covered her bare feet.

'Tara,' he said softly.

She turned and his heart caught again. Never had he seen such sadness in her lovely eyes. Such despair.

'I was going to go before you got back,' she said brokenly. 'I wanted to. Oh, how I wanted to! But in the end, I couldn't. I love you too much, Max. I've always loved you too much.'

When her head dropped into her hands and she began to sob, Max just stood there, appalled. Guilt consumed him that he had brought her to this. But then he stepped forward and put his arms around her shaking shoulders, buoyed by the thought that she would feel happier about loving him once she knew what he had done.

She sagged against him, still weeping.

His heart filled to overflowing as he held her close. Maybe she *did* love him too much. But he loved her just as much. Hell, he was willing to change his whole life for her.

'There, there,' he soothed, and began stroking her hair down her back.

She shuddered, then wrenched herself away from him. Her face jerked up to his, tear-stained but defiant.

'Oh, no, Max. You don't get away with things as easily as that. For once, I want you to explain yourself. I want to know exactly what you've been doing today, every single moment. And don't think you can con your way out of things by telling me you went shopping for an engagement ring. That's what Kate thought, the poor deluded woman. And it might even be true. But that would have taken you all of ten minutes. I can see it now. You'd stride into a jewellery shop and tell the fawning female shop assistant to give you the biggest and the best diamond ring they had.'

Max was ruefully amused by her description of his shopping excursion for a ring. It was startlingly accurate. If the situation wasn't so serious, he might even have laughed.

'You're right and you're wrong, Tara. I did do that,' he confessed. 'But not today. I bought a two-carat rock a week ago. It's been up here in my room all week, waiting to be produced on cue tonight. But I took it back to Sydney today and left it there.'

She blinked, then just stared at him.

'I'm not the same man who bought that ring, Tara. During this past week I realised I didn't want to play lord and master with you any more. That is what

Joyce and Jen used to call me, isn't it? For one thing, I want to take you shopping for a ring and let you pick something *you* like. If you'll still have me, that is.'

'That depends, doesn't it?' she said with a proud toss of her head. 'So what *were* you doing all day today?' she demanded to know. 'As if I don't know. You're back to wearing a business suit. That speaks for itself.'

'I'm wearing a business suit because I spent most of the day in serious negotiations. With your family.'

Tara's mouth fell open.

'You would have already known this if you hadn't taken the phone off the hook. I've been trying to ring you all afternoon. Your mother tried to ring you as well. When the number was engaged, I told her Kate was a real chatterbox to stop her from worrying. But I already suspected what you'd done. I promised to get you to ring her once you knew the good news.'

Tara looked perplexed. 'And what good news would that be?'

'Firstly, I've decided to downsize the Royale chain of hotels. The hotels in Europe will be sold as soon as I can get a reasonable price. But I will go through with the purchase of the hotel in Auckland. I'll also keep our three Asian hotels for now. We'd lose too much if we sold those at this point in time. On top of that, it doesn't take as long to fly over to them. Not that I intend doing as much travelling as I once did. I will be delegating more in future. Naturally, I'll keep the Regency Royale in Sydney, and the penthouse. It's always wise to have a Sydney base. And it will make a good place for breaks away.'

'Breaks away from where?' Tara was looking even more perplexed.

'I'm going to buy a house up here for us to live in. *If* you agree to marry me, of course,' he swiftly added, having to remind himself all the time to keep consulting her feelings. This was the most difficult change for him to embrace. He was too used to being the boss, in not having to consult anyone when making decisions.

'It all came to me when I was out surfing this morning,' he charged on. 'What better place to raise a family, I thought, than Wamberal? Of course, I realised straight away that living up here could cause some logistical problems. You'd be a long way from your mother, and your sister. I, too, would be a long way from *my* parents, who I was surprised to find I really want as part of my life again. Poor old things need my help. Hands-on help. I visited them again this morning and realised my mother could not cope alone much longer. There was only one logical solution. They would all have to move up here, lock, stock and barrel.'

'*All* of them? Move up here?'

'Yep. That's what I've been doing today. Putting that plan into action. Not an easy task to accomplish in so short a time, but I managed to at least get it off the ground.'

'You're not joking, are you?'

'Not at all. Would I joke about something like that? You know, I was surprised just how many places there are on the market up here. We have oodles to choose from. We might not even have to do too much renovating. I was suitably impressed, I can tell you. So what do you think? Are you happy with that idea?'

'What? Why, yes, yes, it's a wonderful idea. But Max...' She reached out to touch his arm. 'Are you really sure that this is what you want?' As her eyes searched his, her surprise changed to wariness, and her hand dropped away. 'You're not just doing this to get me to marry you, are you? I won't wake up after the wedding to find you've changed your mind about all this, will I?'

'Come, now, Tara. Would I be foolish enough to do that? No, my darling, this is what I want, too,' he reassured, taking both her hands in his. 'This last week up here with you has taught me so much. You've made me see how much I've been missing with my crazy, jet-setting lifestyle. I don't want to end up like my father. That's something I vowed I would never do. I want to be an integral part of my family's life, not just living on the fringes of it. I want to be a good husband and father. I don't want to just give lip-service to the roles.'

A strange little smile played around her lips. 'Some

lip-service wouldn't go astray at this point in time,' she murmured.

Max stared into her glittering green eyes, the sexual message in her words distracting him from any further verbal persuasion. Instead, he lifted her hands to his mouth, his eyes never leaving hers as he kissed each knuckle in turn.

'Your wish,' he whispered between kisses, 'is my command.'

'No, your wish is *my* command today. Remember?'

'I'm so glad you reminded me.' He placed her arms up around his neck then bent to scoop her up into his arms. 'Your room or mine?'

She smiled. 'Surprise me.'

'No, don't leave me yet,' Tara pleaded, and pulled Max back down into her arms.

They were in the room where Max had slept alone all week, in the bed where she'd wanted to be every single night.

Oh, how she'd missed him; how she'd missed this.

Her arms tightened around him.

'But I'm heavy,' Max protested. 'Are you sure this won't hurt the baby?'

'Of course not. He's only tiny yet.'

Max levered himself up onto his elbows. '*He?* It might be a girl.'

'No. It's a boy.'

He smiled. 'You could be wrong.'

'I could be. But I'm not.'

He shook his head. 'Your mother said you were stubborn. Which reminds me. I haven't called her yet. Don't go away, now.'

Tara moaned in soft protest when he withdrew.

He bent down to kiss her on the lips, then on each breast before straightening. 'Now, don't you dare cover up. I want you to stay exactly as you are.'

She lay there, happily compliant, whilst Max scrambled off the bed.

'Who dropped all these clothes on the floor?' he complained as he swept up his trousers.

'You did,' she told him, ogling him shamelessly as he stood there in the buff, rifling through his pockets.

There was no doubt that the week up here had done him good in more ways than one. He was looking great.

'I put your mum's number in the memory,' he explained as he whisked out his cellphone and pressed a few buttons.

'Joyce? It's Max. Yes, I'm with Tara and she's thrilled to pieces... What? Oh, yes, she said yes... You did say yes to marrying me, darling, didn't you?' he asked as he lay back down beside her on the bed, making her gasp when his free hand slid between her still-parted legs. 'Yes, she can't wait till you're all living up here... Yes, you're so right... Would you like to talk to her, Joyce? Yep, she's right here. Champing at the bit.'

Tara flushed all over as he handed over the phone.

'Mum,' she said somewhat breathlessly. Max was

right. She *was* champing at the bit. But not for conversation with her mother.

'Isn't Max marvellous?' her mother was saying whilst Tara struggled to ignore the sensations Max was evoking. 'He's going to get me a little house close to yours. And he's going to back Dale in a plumbing business. *And* he's going to give them an interest-free loan for a house. He wanted to buy them one outright but Jen and Dale didn't want that. They want to pay their own way.'

Tara did her best to make all the right remarks whilst her mother rattled on. But it was difficult to concentrate on her mother's revelations about Max's generosity whilst the man himself was doing what he did oh, so well.

OK, so Kate had been right. Max was basically a good man. But he could also be downright wicked.

She had to bite her tongue to stop herself from crying out on one occasion. But she was doing some serious squirming. In the end, she couldn't stand it any more. She had to get her mother off the phone.

'Mum, I hate to cut and run but Max made an early reservation for dinner and I haven't even started getting dressed yet.' And wasn't *that* the truth!

'I understand,' Joyce trilled. 'You'll want to make yourself look extra-nice tonight. Ring me tomorrow, would you, and we'll have a nice long talk?'

'Will do, Mum. And tell Jen I'll ring her, too.'

'Oh, yes. Do that. She's very excited. And so are

the kids. They just love the idea of living near a beach.'

'Must go, Mum,' she said through gritted teeth.

She pressed the phone off just as Max's head lifted.

'Don't you mean you must come?' he quipped when she clicked the phone shut and tossed it away.

'You're a sadist,' she threw at him. 'Oh, God, don't stop.'

He grinned down at her. 'This is my night, remember? Don't go telling me what to do and what not to do.'

'Yes, Max,' she said with a sigh.

'Now, first things first. You do agree to marry me, don't you?'

'Yes, Max.'

'And you agree to all my plans.'

'Yes, Max. Except…'

His eyes narrowed on her. 'Except what?'

'Do you think before I have this baby and before you sell all those lovely hotels in Europe, we could go on a trip together and stay in some of them? I have this fantasy about making love in Paris.'

'Are you sure you're well enough to travel?'

'Absolutely. When I woke this morning, there wasn't a trace of morning sickness.'

'In that case, I would love to take you on an overseas trip. We could make it our honeymoon. My fantasies include making love to you in every big city in the world, not just Paris. But first, I think I need to make love to you right here and now.'

Tara sighed when he rolled her onto her side and slid into her from behind, filling her heart as well as her body.

'Oh, Max,' she cried.

He caressed her breasts whilst he kissed her hair, her ear, her shoulder. 'Have I made you truly happy today at long last, my love?'

'Oh, yes.'

'You will tell me in future if and when I'm doing something wrong. I want to make you happy, Tara.'

'I'm very happy,' she choked out. 'Ooh. I really like making love this way. I think it's my favourite.'

'That's good, because we'll be doing it a lot like this in future. I looked up all the websites on pregnancy last Friday night and came across this really interesting one which listed all the safest and most comfortable positions for making love during a pregnancy. This was number one. We can do it like this till well into the last trimester.'

'There are others?' she said, her voice having taken on a faraway sound.

'There's something for every occasion, and every stage of your pregnancy.' His hands dropped down to caress her belly. 'Frankly, I can't wait till this is all big with my baby.'

'You won't find it unattractive?'

'Are you kidding? It's a real turn-on, touching you like this, knowing my child is inside there. And then there's your breasts. They're already larger, you know.'

'Yes. And very sensitive.'

'So I noticed.'

She gasped when he gave the distended tips a gentle tug.

'I… I seem to be more sensitive all round,' she said. 'My body as well as my emotions. I'm going to need a lot of loving, Max.'

'Don't worry. You'll be loved. But slowly, my love. And gently. We don't want to do anything which might put the baby at risk.'

'No, of course not,' she said, still slightly amazed at how much he wanted this child. 'Do you want more children after this, Max?'

'If this pregnancy is anything to go by, I think I'll keep you having babies for quite a few years. I've never seen you look more beautiful or more sexy than you looked today when I saw you out on that veranda.' He didn't add that he'd never seen her look sadder.

Max vowed that he would never let her look that sad again.

'What about names?' he said. 'Have you picked out any names?'

'No. I thought I'd wait and see what he looks like first.'

'Or what *she* looks like.'

'I told you. It's a boy. Only a boy would cause so much trouble.'

'True.'

'Max…you've stopped moving.'

'If I move, I'll be history. I got myself over-excited.'

Tara laughed. 'In that case, we'll just talk for a while till you calm down.'

'Good idea.'

'Max…'

'Mmm?'

'I want to thank you…for all you did today. I can't tell you how much it means to me that you would go to so much trouble to make me happy.'

'My pleasure, princess.'

'Mum sounded ecstatic as well. I'm sure Jen and Dale are, too. You've been very generous. And I think it's really sweet that you're getting along so well with your folks now. I'll have to go and meet them soon.'

'How about tomorrow?'

'Tomorrow would be fine. What time is it now? We're supposed to be going out to dinner tonight, remember?'

'It's only five to seven,' Max said with a quick glance at his watch. 'How long will it take you to get dressed?'

'Not long.'

'In that case, I think we've talked long enough, don't you think?'

'Absolutely.'

Everyone was relocated to Wamberal before the wedding, which took place on Wamberal Beach in August. Tara was an unashamedly pregnant bride, wearing an original gown that Max had bought her in Paris. They'd enjoyed a two-month pre-wedding holiday travelling all around Europe. Their actual honeymoon was spent at home, decorating the nursery in their comparatively modest new house. Max and Tara had decided together that they wanted a simple lifestyle for their family.

Their son was born a week late. A beautiful, placid, happy baby. They named him Stevie.

The world's bestselling romance series.

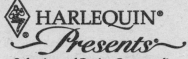

HARLEQUIN®
Presents

Seduction and Passion Guaranteed!

Your dream ticket to the vacation of a lifetime!

Why not relax and allow Harlequin Presents® to whisk you away
to stunning international locations with our new miniseries…

FOREIGN

*Where irresistible men and sophisticated women
surrender to seduction under the golden sun.*

**Don't miss this opportunity to experience glamorous
lifestyles and exotic settings in:**

This Month:
MISTRESS OF CONVENIENCE
by Penny Jordan
on sale August 2004, #2409

Coming Next Month:
IN THE ITALIAN'S BED
by Anne Mather
on sale September 2004, #2416

Don't Miss!
THE MISTRESS WIFE
by Lynne Graham
on sale November 2004, #2428

FOREIGN AFFAIRS… A world full of passion!

**Pick up a Harlequin Presents® novel and you will enter a world
of spine-tingling passion and provocative, tantalizing romance!**

Available wherever Harlequin books are sold.

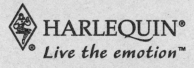

HARLEQUIN®
Live the emotion™

www.eHarlequin.com   HPFAUPD

Receive a FREE hardcover book from

H A R L E Q U I N   R O M A N C E®

in September!

Harlequin Romance celebrates the launch of the line's new cover design by offering you this exclusive offer valid only in September, only in Harlequin Romance.

To receive your
FREE HARDCOVER BOOK
written by bestselling author
Emilie Richards, send us four
proofs of purchase from any
September 2004 Harlequin
Romance books. Further details
and proofs of purchase can be
found in all September 2004
Harlequin Romance books.

*Must be postmarked
no later than October 31.*

**Don't forget to be one of the first
to pick up a copy of the new-look
Harlequin Romance novels in September!**

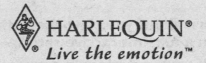

Visit us at www.eHarlequin.com

HRPOP0904

The world's bestselling romance series.

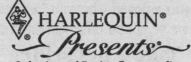

HARLEQUIN®
Presents

Seduction and Passion Guaranteed!

THE PRINCESS BRIDES

For duty, for money…for passion!

Discover a thrilling new trilogy from a rising star of Harlequin Presents®, Jane Porter!

Meet the Royals…

Chantal, Nicolette and Joelle are members of the blue-blooded Ducasse family. Step inside their sophisticated and glamorous world and watch as these beautiful princesses find they have to marry three international playboys—for duty, for money… and definitely for passion!

Don't miss

THE SULTAN'S BOUGHT BRIDE (#2418)
September 2004

THE GREEK'S ROYAL MISTRESS (#2424)
October 2004

THE ITALIAN'S VIRGIN PRINCESS (#2430)
November 2004

Pick up a Harlequin Presents® novel and you will enter a world of spine-tingling passion and provocative, tantalizing romance!

Available wherever Harlequin books are sold.

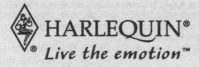

HARLEQUIN®
Live the emotion™

www.eHarlequin.com